CROWFALL

Published in the UK by Scholastic, 2021
Euston House, 24 Eversholt Street, London, NW1 1DB
Scholastic Ireland, 89E Lagan Road, Dublin
Industrial Estate, Glasnevin, Dublin, D11 HP5F

Copyright © Vasthi Hardy, 2021
Cover illustration by George Ermos
Map illustrations by Jamie Gregory

The right of Vasthi Hardy to be identified
as the author of this work has been asserted by her
under the Copyright, Designs and Patents Act 1988.

ISBN 978 1407 19727 2

A CIP catalogue record for this book
is available from the British Library.

Printed by CPI Group (UK) Ltd, Croydon, CR0 4YY

Paper made from wood grown in sustainable forests
and other controlled sources.

1 3 5 7 9 10 8 6 4 2

www.scholastic.co.uk

FOR IMOGEN

TRONHOLD TIME UNIT	EQUIVALENT
Day	24 hours
Deciday (1/10th of a day)	2 hours and 24 minutes
Centiday (1/100th of a day)	14 minutes and 24 seconds
Milliday (1/1000th of a day)	1 minute and 26 seconds

CHAPTER 1

The storm appeared without warning.

Morbid clouds moved over the horizon, eclipsing the distant blue as though an enormous blanket was being pulled across the sky. One milliday Orin Crowfall was gazing at the cobalt sea, then it became muddy green, and in no time at all, it was an angry brown, and the breeze had become powerful enough to ruffle his cropped brown hair. The storm was heading towards Ironhold, and as bad luck would have it, Orin was currently clinging to the edge of the West Tip cliffs. Arms and legs slender as scaffold poles were pressed against the cold limestone, and one hand, strong for a twelve-year-old boy, clung on to a steel buttress, the other hand shielding his eyes from the sun.

Cody fluttered up from below. "Do you see that?" Her large robotic eyes shone out of her round face, black and serious. She was around a quarter of the size of Orin, standard size for a fixie, but different from other fixies in many ways. The orange glow of the late afternoon light reflected off her, tipping the silver of her double antennae, curved shoulders and flickering wings.

"You'd have to be buried underground not to see that beast," Orin said, glancing back at the storm.

"We should head back."

Orin looked down at the broken juniper sapling growing against odds between the metal fortifications that braced the crumbling cliff. There hadn't been a natural juniper tree discovered on Ironhold in three years. Of course, they had some growing in the botanical gardens, but not in the wild. This tree wouldn't survive another storm. Orin had been carefully digging it out for the past three centidays, which was delicate work due to the roots being tangled between rock and metal, but he was almost done. "We have enough time to save it."

Cody frowned and glanced at the thin strip of beach far below them, which was still strewn with the remains of an unfortunate West Tip box house, a victim of the last storm. "The clouds are only a centiday away if we're lucky. I'd rather that wasn't us." She pointed at the wreckage.

"Then that's a centiday we have to save this tree and get back up top."

"You're incorrigible, Orin Crowfall."

"And you use big words for a fixie." He grinned despite the chill now embedded in his stomach at the sight of the impending storm. There had been too many lately. "We have time," Orin repeated, glancing at the waves now churning furiously. He wasn't going to let this plant die. He blew out a long breath. His rope and harness were frayed and his safety would be more of a wish than a certainty if he found himself in trouble, but he was a strong climber. Since he was four, he'd scoured the edges of Ironhold, collecting extra scraps of food: limpets, seaweed, clams, sea lettuce – anything to supplement the sparse quota received by his family and other West Tippers. But mostly, this was where sometimes, just sometimes, a new plant could be found: a rare seed blown in on a distant wind, or a sapling fighting to survive, like this very juniper. He'd mend and nurture them for a while, before taking the plants to be logged at the cultivation towers in exchange for credits, which his family could use for food. It was the way of Ironhold that everything had a system.

Doubling his speed, Orin carried on with the task of saving the tiny tree. Cody flew to the far side, flipped open one of her fingers and extended a small whirring tool to the rocks around the root.

"Be careful, too much vibration might snap it." The main stem was spliced, meaning the small tree's life hung in the balance.

"I am being careful. But we *really* shouldn't be doing this now."

It had been hot when Orin had left the Engineerium, the island of Ironhold drowsy with afternoon sun, but now the wind howled ominously and the chill air seeped into his skin and burrowed into his bones. He regretted wearing a thin shirt and not bringing his cape. The weather could change within a moment on Ironhold these days; sunshine to storm, mild to gale, blue to grey, warmth to frost.

Above, the small box houses of West Tip teetered precariously, wood and metal groaning in the breeze. Some of the buildings right on the edge had been abandoned by the people lucky enough to have friends or relatives further inland, but many were still occupied, Orin's own home included, which was now only a few steps from crumbling into the ocean.

Things were harder in West Tip than the rest of Ironhold, being the poorest area of the island. Everyone in West Tip had either grown up there and never managed to move out or, like Orin's family, had committed some crime against the rules of Ironhold and been moved there. Built on a rocky outcrop, it was a maze of straight bridges and simple square buildings stacked on top of each other on any available nook, external stairways tracing the walls. West Tip was still in the orderly tradition of Ironhold, with precise lines and angles, but there was a precarious nature to the order of the buildings. Everything looked as though, if you were to take out one piece, it would all tumble like a child's toy building blocks, and that was without the threat of a storm.

Taking a deep breath, Orin pushed with his feet, then thrust his body around and underneath the juniper's mid-section. Ensuring he had a secure grip on one of the metal scaffolds, he reached to his belt for some tape, pulled off a strip and began carefully wrapping the broken stem.

"I guess no crows will be returning today," he called to Cody.

"Seeing as there haven't been any crows on Ironhold since before both our lifetimes, I'd say the chances are still somewhere between zero and nothing."

With a quick glance below, Orin could see that the waves coming on to the small beach were already choppier and the light had changed as though time were accelerating towards late evening. The storm was almost upon them, its thick, churning mass rolling hungrily their way. The chill inside of him turned to ice as he realized there was no time. A sudden fierce wind rushed at them, stealing the breath from Orin's lungs. The muscles in his hands and feet clenched, gripping rock and metal as the gust attacked them. A loud *clang* sounded as Cody was thrust into the cliff.

"Hold on to something!" he shouted.

"You too!" she called back, although her robotic voice snagged in the blast of air.

Distant wind chimes rang feverishly above.

Biting his lip, Orin pulled himself into the cliff, arcing his body around the juniper to protect it.

The wind abated.

He glanced across to Cody. "Are you all right?"

She nodded. "A centiday was too optimistic. Orin, we need to get off the cliff, *now*."

"But the juniper is almost free. The credits will be good and—"

"—and you just can't help fixing things, I know."

Cody was right; it was about more than credits. He couldn't stand the thought of seeing something broken and not trying to mend it. He didn't know why; Cody said it was because he was a fixie like her at heart, but there was more to it. Somehow it made him feel more part of the world, part of nature. It made him feel like *someone*, not just a boy from West Tip who was destined to serve the engineers for the rest of his life.

Lightning lit the sky in a double flash, reflecting spectacularly off Cody's body and quad wing-blades. Thunder growled moments after. With renewed vigour, Orin released the last of the main roots.

"Orin, *now*," Cody urged. "I had you down as an intelligent human – don't prove me wrong."

"Here, you take the plant home and wait for me there."

She fluttered in front of him. "I don't think I should leave you."

"I'll be fine, only a milliday behind."

Frowning, Cody clasped the young juniper tree between her small metallic hands. For a moment, she hovered uncomfortably, then, with a flicker, she flew upwards and Orin began his journey back up the cliff face, clipping in his carabiner to the next rope. He was barely halfway when the clouds drew in. The water below turned black and the sky opened, unleashing furious rain. For a moment, Orin clung to the rocks as he was pounded by the wind, and water splattered the metal poles and rocks around him, drenching his shirt and shorts. But he knew that staying here would mean certain death. Sirens punctured the thunder as messenger-bots flew the streets of Ironhold, alerting the population that it was time to shelter and batten down. Distant rumbling and grinding signalled the Ironhold storm shelters heaving into place, and great lightning rods whirred into the sky.

It was so dark now that Orin could barely see where to clip in, or the next hand- and foothold.

Sweat poured down his face, mixed with rain as he drove onwards. Fighting the wind was arm-wrenching work, and he was soon shaking with tiredness. Tiny flecks of ice within the droplets meant the rain bit when it hit him, as though he was being bombarded by grit. Unable to see, he grabbed at rocks and tried to rely on the familiarity of the route, but in reality he didn't know if he was still some distance from the top, or inches. He just had to keep pushing on.

With a boom that shook every cell in his body, thunder crashed directly overhead; lightning had hit the nearest rod. His heart leapt. The cliff shook violently, and the piece of rock he clung to trembled and began crumbling beneath his grip. Panic erupted hot and deadly as his hands fell away from the cliff along with the rocks. His stomach lurched as though it had been yanked to the top of his chest as he began to drop. But it was OK. There was the rope; he would be all right and his harness *would* hold. Flailing to grab anything he could, his hands found rope, then with heart-stopping realization, he knew it was loose and tumbling down along with his body.

He was falling.

CHAPTER 2

Ironhold, resplendent with its imposing towers and technology, raised its storm defence shields and rods and stood firm, protecting its residents from the attacking storm. But on the west side, the tiny figure of Orin Crowfall tumbled from the cliff edge towards the ocean.

Shutting his eyes, all Orin could hope for was that he'd be blown into the water instead of the jagged rocks below.

Lightning flashed silver. A blur of wings and two beaming eyes rushed towards him. With a bone-wrenching jerk, his waist yanked and his body slammed into ice-cold iron and rock. Cody was holding the last bit of rope. "Orin, grab something! I can't take your weight for long!"

With every piece of energy he could muster, Orin reached for the cliff, finding two handholds and juts for his feet. "I'm all right!" he called. But the rocks were slippery and he wasn't sure how long he could hold on.

"I've still got the rope, but the maintenance ladder should be to the right. Follow my lights. It's not far!"

The wind and rain hammered as Orin fought his way across the rocks. His hand met a cold rung of the ladder. He looped it with an arm, sucked a deep breath and began climbing. Lightning was now fast and frequent, the wind and rain relentless.

A flash illuminated a sign marked DANGER, and with a rush of relief, Orin knew he was just a few steps from the top. He hauled himself over to level ground.

Trembling, he collapsed on his back in a puddle, his chest heaving. The sky above blazed and thundered.

Cody put a metal hand to his head. "Humans are reckless. None so more than you."

"Thanks for coming back," he panted. Any other fixie robot would have followed the instructions to go home and thought nothing of it.

"Your body temperature is low."

"Orin, is that you?" Footsteps splashed his way.

Cody's lights dimmed and she became still as Orin scrambled to his feet; he knew that voice, kind and always with an edge of concern.

"Mum?" Orin called above the wailing wind.

A beam of torchlight bounced towards him.

"Orin, thank goodness. I've been scouring the streets for you! Can't you see there's a storm?" Mum loomed above, her deep brown eyes creased at the edges, rain dripping from her brown curls and short cape.

"I was on my way back from the Engineerium and I, er, tripped." Mum and Dad hated him climbing on the cliff, even in fair weather.

Mum tilted her head and her eyes narrowed. A trickle of rain ran down the scar that cut through one of her straight eyebrows, an injury from working in the recycling plant once. She sighed and reached a soggy gloved hand out to Orin, fingertips poking through the ends. "Come on. Let's get inside before you freeze solid!"

Trying to hide the shaking in his bones from the

fall and cold, Orin grasped her hand. She pulled him up with strength and care, two things that Mum always managed in everything she did. Cody sometimes remarked they were traits Orin had inherited. He scooped Cody up in his arms.

They hurried through several of the thin, linear alleys towards home, rain gushing from the flat square roofs in waterfall-like sheets, their feet sploshing through puddles already ankle deep in places. Mum's khaki trousers were already wet through, as were his own clothes.

"You shouldn't be bringing a fixie along to the Engineerium. You're incredibly lucky to have been asked to be a server. I don't want you to risk your place by being distracted," said Mum, her voice loud in an attempt to combat the wind and rain.

"It's fine. She waits outside."

Cody threw him a quick wink.

They burst through the door and secured the latches behind them, then stood dripping pools on to the floor. Dad and Grandpa looked over from the two armchairs where they sat huddled around the fire. Buttery light glimmered on their anxious faces, and Dad's copper hair shone as brightly as the fire.

Grandpa relaxed back into his chair as soon as he saw Orin was all right and grinned in relief.

"Orin, what happened to you?" asked Dad, jumping up.

Orin's arms and legs were burning with scratches. He shrugged. "I slipped in the rain."

Swiftly Dad grabbed a knitted blanket from a basket beside Grandpa's armchair and wrapped it around Orin. "Get beside the fire, you're drenched. Estri, you should get changed. The storm shutters are up and all we can do is wait it out."

"I'll dry out by the fire after I've boiled some water," said Mum, hanging up her sodden cape.

Outside, the wind howled and battered around the house as though a great monster surged through the streets, squeezing the bones out of everything it passed. Orin knelt in front of the fireplace between the armchairs. They felt so out of place compared to the angular, practical shapes of all the regular Ironhold-supplied furniture, but Orin loved the colours and warmth they brought to the room. Grandpa loved to knit, using fabric created from recycled plastic he found up at the plant, and little by little he'd customized what had once been two grey standard-issue chairs into something that felt like home. Orin put Cody beside him to dry out her mechanisms a little. She was made of a material called azothe, which was resilient and flexible, with good temperature control, but there was an organic part of her that wasn't regulation and he wasn't sure how that would fare if it got too damp.

"I'll get you some dry clothes. Lucky I just washed your spare set," said Dad, ruffling Orin's hair, then hurrying to a cupboard, while Mum steadily made her special cocoa. It wasn't real cocoa – they hadn't had that since he was four – but she always made it when there was a storm, and it included some of the honey-mead that Grandpa had made with his friend Bartley, who worked in the bee tower. Dad always showed his worries with expressive hand gestures and by pacing the room, especially in big storms, while Mum was more measured in her movements, only showing her concern through the tone of her voice. Orin was glad he'd inherited his mum's steadiness, without which he certainly wouldn't have been a good climber.

Grandpa squeezed Orin's shoulder, then leant in and gave Orin a quick smile, his round cheeks and large nose flushed with warmth from the fire, his moustache ends twiddled into curls. "That's a lot of scratches," he whispered. "I wonder where you were, exactly, when you slipped." Grandpa had taught him to climb when they'd moved to West Tip, and although he couldn't come with Orin any more because of his bad knees, Grandpa understood the thrill of climbing – unlike Orin's parents.

"It was the juniper, Grandpa, the one I told you about yesterday. We saved it," said Orin with a quick glance to Mum to make sure she wasn't listening.

Grandpa smiled. "Grandma would be proud of you, you know. You're so like her: obsessed by growing plants and finding new ones. You have the round face of your father, your mother's dark hair, but most of all I see Grandma in you. The care … the wildness … the glint of adventure in the eye." After a moment, Grandpa focused back on Orin, but his face crumpled with concern. "Perhaps you're too much like her."

Orin put a reassuring hand on Grandpa's. "What did I inherit from you?"

Grandpa's face lit up once more. He clenched his fist and pointed at a bicep. "I was a good climber once, too. Let's hope you don't get my dodgy knees, though!"

Then Mum was beside them with the steaming cocoa. Brown and milky, and when Orin swallowed it a burst of fire in his throat made him want to cough; but it was good, and it warmed him from the inside.

"Put the evening transmission on, Dad," said Mum, sitting in the other armchair and rubbing her curls with a towel. "I want to see if the Core engineers have calculated that the winds will get worse."

Grandpa reached over to the small metal box on the table beside him. He swiped his hand across the word *IRONCOM*, which was marked on the top, and it lit with white light. A voice Orin recognized as that of one of the Core engineers, Silver Blecher, sounded from the box. "—cumulonimbus currently twenty ironspans high, but still growing. Easterly gusts of eighty-seven ironspans per deciday in West Tip. Tornado columns have not been detected, but all residents of Ironhold are ordered to stay indoors."

Dad passed Orin clean pyjamas. "There's no chance the storm will pass this evening, so you may as well go straight for these. Off you go – you'd best get properly dry, or you'll catch a nasty chill." He stared at Orin expectantly, his wild hair looking like he'd been the one caught in a storm.

"Thanks, Dad." Orin scooped up Cody, went to his bedroom and shut the door, placing her on his bed.

Orin's room was small, with a bed cobbled together from repurposed produce crates topped with layers of Grandpa's home-sewn quilts and bright knitted blankets. The remaining space was filled with jars, pots and glass containers of all shapes and sizes housing tiny indoor gardens, shoots being nurtured, weather-worn plants being restored to health, home-made growth tonics, and the like. They balanced on every available surface: shelves, the window ledge and most of the floor.

"Are your circuits all right?" he whispered.

"Yes, my power source seems pretty resilient to water," she said quietly. They always whispered at home because it was a secret that Cody could talk as well as a person could. Other fixies spoke in simple commands like *affirmative* and *negative*, but she was different.

"Hmm. Well, maybe you should stay at home tomorrow and rest it. Just in case."

"If you insist. But I'm sure it'll just need its usual nightly resting time." She shrugged, then fluttered out of his arms to land on the floor.

When Orin was a small boy, he had called fixies "fairies", because they'd seemed so magical with their silvery skin and wings. Even now he thought it was a good way to describe them: metallic fairies.

"It looks like the juniper will survive, at least," she said, pointing to the small tree placed carefully beneath the window.

"Yeah, thanks for bringing it back. How did you get it inside without Mum or Dad seeing?"

"I came in through the back window."

"And thanks for saving me too." He sat on the floor, pulled out Cody's bed – a small crate on wheels where she went at night to rest her power source – and began searching under his bed for a box of earth for the tree. He moved aside his small container of clothes, then became aware that Cody had flown back to stand beside him.

"Orin, you could've died. You would have, if I hadn't come back." Cody's antennae trembled.

"Well, now we're even; I saved you from being scrapped, and you just saved me."

"Does that mean I'm free from service and can go off to explore the world?" she said with a wink.

The thought of Cody not being around felt like an empty pit had opened in his stomach. "Only if you take me with you." He smiled. "Besides, this isn't service; you're free to go at any time, or rejoin the other fixies."

"Yeah, right, and talk in single answers all day until I die of boredom? Besides, how can I leave you to the mercy of your human incapability? For a start, I'm a quarter of your size yet twice as strong, and don't get me started on brainpower."

"All right, all right, enough of the gloating," he laughed.

It had been three years ago that Orin had found Cody at the recycling plant. He'd been looking for chipped pots or jars to use for seeds and had found a broken fixie among a heap of junk. He couldn't bear to think of a fixie being melted down, so he'd begged one of the engineers to let him take her to try and mend. The engineer had taken pity, and agreed on the understanding that if Orin couldn't fix it, he would return it. Orin never gave up on fixing anything, but he almost had with Cody. He'd fixed most of her tools, even modified a few, but he couldn't get a new battery because they cost too many credits ... until he'd found an alternative power source at the Engineerium that seemed to be just the thing. But when he'd got her working again, she wasn't like the other fixies. She had a personality, her voice was warmer than the standard robotic tones, and she liked to laugh and had opinions. She was even sarcastic! He decided to keep her real self a secret, even from his family, for fear she would be taken away. Between the two of them, they'd agreed she would behave like all the other fixies in the company of others: a knee-high robot who could respond with simple vocabulary, take instructions, and was only programmed to fix things.

Orin took some soil from the chest under his bed, cupped a little into a box, placed the juniper inside and scooped a few more handfuls in. "It's not much, but—"

"—it's home now," Cody finished.

They were the words Mum had said when the family had arrived in West Tip. He had only been four, yet he could remember it as clearly as yesterday. They were the words he'd first spoken when Cody had woken, the words he spoke to every plant he nurtured.

Cody remembered everything in great detail, word for word, as precise as a razor. She smiled at him. Although other fixies didn't use facial expressions, the flexibility in her azothe allowed movement, and Cody liked to use her face to frown, grin, grimace and mirror the myriad human expressions possible.

The shutters on Orin's bedroom window rattled as though someone was outside thumping them. At times like this, Orin was glad they lived in the bottom living cube of the stack. If it was loud down here, it would be terrifying three blocks above. "I've never seen a storm come in this fast," he said.

"That's the fourth one this month."

"I know. I wonder what's causing them." He caught a glimpse of Grandma's book tucked underneath his bed. He'd discovered it in Grandpa's cupboard, where he'd been playing hide-and-seek. Grandpa had found him with it and said he could take it and read it whenever he liked. But Grandpa also warned Orin not to mention it to anyone, as the Ironhold engineers hadn't agreed with Grandma, a talented engineer herself, spending so much time thinking about what might be outside of Ironhold.

Orin loved the book's pictures of crows, and the stories that insisted there were worlds of adventure beyond Ironhold. Everyone on the island was taught that you could sail from one side of the globe to the other and never cross paths with another island, but in the book Grandma had written, there were tales about as many other islands as rivets in the hydro-filter tanks: old islands lost to the sea, new islands grown from volcanic eruptions, even islands of metal that had come from the sky, which Orin was particularly fascinated by. Grandpa said most of the stories had been handed down from generation to generation, but some tales were about places Grandma had seen with her own eyes. Stories of beyond were banned in Ironhold; their island was all by itself in the world, and that suited everyone, because on Ironhold they had engineered everything to perfection – strangers from somewhere else would surely only threaten and steal from them.

Orin flicked to the page with the crows.

Grandma had written in capital letters: *CROWS BRING CHANGE, THE FULFILMENT OF DESTINY*. Beneath these words she'd sketched the crows flying: soaring and swooping, from all angles, magical threads of blue glistening through their black feathers. Their eyes seemed to watch him from the page, wise and knowing, calling to him. They were creatures entwined with his family; their very name, Crowfall, was linked to them. But the name's history wasn't one Orin felt proud of. He wondered how Grandma had felt about *that* story. He ran his fingers over the image. Crows had lived on Ironhold once, and now they had gone – perhaps to explore new places, new islands, places he might go one day too. He flicked to the back of the book where Grandma had sketched herself and written: *This book belongs to Merina Crowfall*. Grandpa was right. It wasn't just the dark hair and round, wide-set eyes that were similar to both himself and Mum. There was an inner spark in her expression: a yearning for more than she had. He knew that look, because he saw it whenever he looked in the mirror.

CHAPTER 3

The following morning it felt as though the storm had merely been a bad dream. A sliver of bright sun shone through the living space window, casting a beam on to the concrete floor. Mum and Dad were up and dressed in their khaki trousers and brown jumpers ready for work, making breakfast in the small kitchen area, while Grandpa was still snoring in his room.

"Turn on the morning transmission, it's about to start," Dad called over.

Orin swiped his hand over the IRONCOM box, which lit with white light. After a few moments, the rhythmic sound of turning cogs churned and a low whistle sounded, signifying the start of the transmission. Then a monotone robotic voice spoke, the standard voice of Ironcom.

"Your morning transmission is brought to you by Ironcom – keeping the citizens of Ironhold informed and connected."

An image of Commander Vida Forge projected into the space above the Ironcom box. She wore her lead engineer uniform of white suit and trousers with a matching long cape, pinned with the metal symbol of Ironhold, an upside-down V with four nails splicing through it. The shoulders of her pristine cape were adorned with intricate metal epaulettes made of bladed layers of iron shards, so thin they looked like feathers.

The majority of transmissions were given by the other members of the Core, but after a big storm, Commander Forge always addressed the people directly. The citizens looked to her for reassurance after such an event, and she never failed to show that through technology, the engineers of Ironhold were absolutely in control of whatever the elements could throw at them.

Her face was composed, her jawline set firmly, chin slightly raised, skin luminous like glass, her steel-blue eyes fixed and confident. Orin always admired the way Vida Forge could make you feel as though she was speaking to you personally, even though she was addressing thousands. She was young for a leader – younger than Mum, Orin guessed, although he couldn't be sure. There were a few moments of silence before Commander Forge spoke, which Orin had noticed she did often, the pause adding weight to the words about to be uttered.

"Good morning. I can report that yet again there have been no casualties of the storm." Her voice was as measured and reassuring as her appearance. "All buildings remain strong thanks to the excellent advancements in our island protection. The fixies are busily repairing the minimal damage to the city. All sectors are on full functioning status, and all duties can continue as usual today. Your safety is the Core's priority." She placed a hand on her heart, then gestured out, as though addressing every citizen. "Remember: industry brings prosperity."

"Industry brings prosperity," Dad repeated.

Mum laughed. "You don't have to say it at home, Caelan."

"Force of habit." He kissed her on the cheek.

Cody sneakily pursed her lips in a big pout, and Orin tried not to laugh.

The transmission continued with the usual updates on quotas and production, plus news on Engineerium advancements and appointments, which Orin always found to be rather dull, so he decided to leave for work early. He put Cody in his room, said goodbye to his parents, and left for the under-rail.

Several of the West Tip houses were looking worse for wear, with broken shutters and lolling drainpipes, but in the glimpses between the square, stacked structures of West Tip, the various towers and buildings of Ironhold patterned the skyline in their usual way, strong and secure.

Orin admired what Ironhold stood for with its invention and order, but his heart tugged elsewhere. To the sea. To far-off islands and adventure. To something *different*. As he jogged through the thin alleys of West Tip, he looked to the clear sky of the new day. He imagined crows soaring through the blue, a sign that there were other islands with creatures and plants just waiting to be discovered. That there was more for him than serving breakfast to engineers and clearing the plates afterwards. That he could create a new tale, one to eclipse the sad story of his surname.

But people weren't meant to think about anything out there, beyond. Commander Forge said that Ironhold needed everyone's focus to keep it strong. And big dreams certainly weren't meant for people from West Tip.

Orin hurried through the streets to the under-rail on his way to serve at the Engineerium before school. There weren't many people around this early, mostly West Tippers in their khaki trousers and brown capes, some with tools attached to belts and duffel bags of equipment for general maintenance and cleaning duties. On the edge of West Tip he came to the under-rail station and walked down the steps behind a tall cultivator in a green cape. Of all the jobs in Ironhold, he thought that cultivating would be the best, but it was highly unlikely that a boy from West Tip could ever do that. West Tippers went into cleaning and maintenance: that was the way it was. Warm air rushed through the tunnel, the pristine white train arrived, and Orin hopped on.

He planned to set up breakfast early and then

head to the library to see if he could find out more about caring for the juniper tree. He could get away with nurturing it himself for a short time, but then he'd have to pass it over to the cultivators; the rule was that new finds had to be surrendered and logged within a week.

The under-rail train stopped at the education sector, where a purple-cloaked professor Orin recognized as Ambrosius Wells stepped off and a couple more green capes got on; then they stopped at the cultivation towers, where all the green capes stepped off; next the library, where two young grey-cloaked standard engineers got on; then the botanical gardens, and finally his stop: the Engineerium, situated at the centre of the island. He hurried up the stairs and emerged from the under-rail in front of the Engineerium. The building's sheer size and beauty never failed to take his breath away. It was nothing short of spectacular. The island's tallest tower, it looked as though enormous crystals had grown up from the ground in crown-like formation topped with silver spires. It was a mostly glass structure with iron veins engineered to transform into panels for storm protection, and crystal lifts weaving in and out of the walls. The base of the Engineerium was so wide that it took a whole milliday to cross from side to side, which Orin knew because he'd borrowed a multi-calc from one of the store cupboards and timed it once. The inside had a large atrium, and above that was a marvellous maze of laboratories, meeting rooms, lecture theatres, offices, equipment stores and the like. The position of a server meant being seen when you were wanted and being invisible as air when you weren't, so Orin had discovered many hidden passageways, interlinking vents and channels, some commonly used by other servers to get from the kitchens to the dining hall and other rooms, and others that were not. Some secret places he just couldn't help exploring.

Orin swiped his pass, went through the automatic doors of the servers' entrance, stepped inside one of the glass lifts and pressed for floor fifty, where he would serve breakfast in the morning and then dinner in the evening before heading home. As he rose, the whole island came into view. Like enormous metal warriors protecting their realm, the many towers of Ironhold stood amid the vast ocean. It wasn't a large island, but every inch had a purpose. Everywhere was invention: the numerous glass cultivation towers in the south; the metallic domes of the education sector in the south-west where the children went to school, and, if you were lucky and talented enough, you went on to train as an engineer; the library to the south-west, a great glass pyramid; the fixie factory to the north-west, with sweeping silver curves and spires; the fat hydro-filter towers with their fountains in the east; the thin straight towers of the power and recycling plants to the north; the rising mid-district offices and engineering labs surrounded by the botanical gardens. Then, at the middle of it all, the Engineerium, the glory of Ironhold, where the most important engineers worked, including their esteemed leader, Commander Vida Forge.

Undeniably, Ironhold was a place of wonder, though it was what lay inside, at the centre of it all, that Orin thought was most incredible.

At the heart, in the very depths of the Engineerium, was a huge living creature.

The Eard.

CHAPTER 4

As high as the Engineerium tower rose into the sky, it was rumoured that the Eard extended the same distance into the ground, with roots reaching far and deep into the island. Few people ever saw the Eard with their own eyes; it was kept far out of sight, sacred to the ten engineers who were the most important officials and brains of the island, known as the Core.

But when Orin had discovered he could navigate the vents, he hadn't been able to resist sneaking around the Engineerium one day, a few months after he'd started working there, and stealing a look below ground for himself. In the centre of the enormous atrium of the building's ground floor was a large glass conservatory surrounded by a sunken moat filled with various pipes and cogs, the inner workings of the Engineerium. An iron walkway led from the hustle and bustle of the main atrium floor, across the pipes and workings over to the conservatory. Only Vida Forge and the Core were allowed inside the glass dome, because that's where the Eard was. Orin had hidden in the vents after duties, then, when everyone had gone, he'd climbed through the pipes to see what he could through the glass. That's when he'd found a gap big enough to crawl through where one of the pipes crossed into the glass wall of the conservatory.

At first the plants inside the conservatory had looked to Orin like any others, if a bit unusual in the different shapes of their leaves. Then he realized they were all connected! Just as he thought he'd found where one plant ended, it continued on as another began.

And not only that, the plants – or plant – could *move*. The Eard was a creature as ancient as the island, and it had the ability to shape itself and grow in all manner of ways.

After the first time Orin slipped inside, it became

easy and he found himself coming back more and more. Sometimes, he'd caught a glimpse of the Eard moving; a flower might bloom spontaneously in Orin's path, or leaves might shiver and change colour. These things happened the more he crept down there, as though the Eard was getting used to him. This was where Orin had found the curious electrical pod that he'd used instead of a battery to power Cody, growing heavy on a vine in a corner, ready for picking.

Orin knew it was dangerous to sneak around the Engineerium outside of work; but, like climbing the cliffs, he couldn't help himself. If anyone discovered what he was doing, it would bring all sorts of trouble for his family. He knew all that, but even still, somehow curiosity always took over. And today he had brought something that might help the Eard. He would visit it later.

The lift announced floor fifty and the doors opened. The corridors of the Engineerium were silent this early, and Orin found himself stepping softly, feeling, as he often did, that he was somewhere he wasn't really meant to be. Most of the other servers were older and from different areas of Ironhold. The adults of West Tip were assigned maintenance and cleaning duties, and the children were at school, unless their parents insisted they help with the work instead. Mum and Dad had made Orin apply for this job and offer his time for free, hoping it would be a route out of West Tip if he worked hard.

So here he was, a boy from West Tip with the honour of serving the most important person on the island: Commander Vida Forge. Working here and running errands for Commander Forge meant Orin missed a lot of school, so it was hard to make and keep friends. At least he had Cody.

From what Orin had been told at school, the Eard was integral to Ironhold, its roots extending far and wide, providing the very foundations to the island, keeping it strong. Without it, it was said that Ironhold would crumble into the sea. For that reason, what could be seen of it above ground was protected by the engineers, and one engineer in particular: Commander Forge. Only she truly had an understanding of the Eard because what made it even more special was that it had a unique connection with particular humans, a bond built over many years.

The Eard always chose a custodian, someone it

could communicate with and connect with, and that person bore a symbol emblazoned on the palm of their hand, known as the mark. The custodian was the leader of the island, the only person allowed to communicate with the Eard. During Orin's lifetime it had only been Commander Forge. As custodian, she ensured that the Eard felt protected at all times, and in return it would grow food supplies just for her and the Core: Orin had served all sorts to Commander Forge, a variety of strange fruits he didn't even know the names of. It was said they grew spontaneously and in a matter of moments, like magic. They weren't plentiful, but even so, Commander Forge conducted a monthly Ironhold lottery for one very lucky person to win one of the fruits grown by the Eard. Orin had always longed to win, but no one in his family ever had. He'd sometimes seen the fruits grow when he was sneaking, but he was careful to leave them, no matter how tempting; he'd felt lucky enough for getting away with taking the pod.

He approached room 505, the main room used for meetings of the Core. Usually, he arrived first to set the table for breakfast, and Commander Forge would arrive at eight o'clock promptly, along with the other engineers.

As Orin was about to push open the door, he noticed through the small round porthole window that Forge was already in the room. She was facing the other direction, unaware of his presence, her long auburn hair plaited with silver thread at the top, then cascading in neat waves down the back of her white cloak. There was something thoughtful in her statuesque posture; he wondered if he should knock and enter or wait quietly for a moment or two. He was early, after all.

One of her robot guards appeared in view and approached her. These strong-bodied, steel-grey robots were slightly taller than humans, and less sophisticated than fixies with their technical capabilities, more like empty, featureless human-shaped metal shells. They could be programmed to perform repetitive tasks, but their basic function was to protect Ironhold, especially its top engineers. Grandpa said there was a whole army of them hidden beneath the city somewhere, ready to protect the island and its precious resources and technologies, should outsiders ever break through the defences. The robot placed a smaller, palm-sized robot, which Orin recognized as a medi-bot, on the table beside

Commander Forge.

Forge extended her hand towards the medi-bot. The medi-bot extended a needle, but Orin's view became obscured as the robot guard stepped back, and he couldn't see any more. He hoped there was nothing wrong with Commander Forge, or the mark on her hand. Ironhold depended on it, after all.

After a milliday, the robot guard stepped forward again and took the medi-bot away. Forge walked towards the far wall. Orin watched, mesmerized, as she pressed a panel and a door swung open, revealing shelves full of old books. He had served the commander almost every day for three years in this room and Orin had no idea that cupboard existed. It was difficult to see from a distance, but the books weren't white and pristine like those in the Ironhold library; these appeared to be tatty and colourful, more like ... Grandma's book. Forge selected one and began leafing through. He wondered what they could be – valuable ancient engineering texts, perhaps?

Then Commander Forge suddenly turned and stared straight at him. Swiftly, he dropped away from the window, but Forge's eyes, as bright as blue stars, were still in his mind.

The door opened.

"Master Crowfall. How long have you been there?" Her voice was unsurprised but curious. There was that measured way of talking, putting you at ease with her calm, absolute authority.

"I. . ." He couldn't help feeling he'd intruded on something he wasn't meant to see, and he wanted the ground to swallow him up.

"You're early. Did the storm make you restless?"

He nodded and tried his best to look innocent.

"You must look at me when I'm talking to you."

He turned his gaze to the commander. She had a youthful face, but he had no idea how old she was, only that she'd ruled longer than he'd been alive, and according to Grandpa she'd invented the mechanical sea monster which had been protecting the island for the past twenty years. The Core called it the Sentinel, but most people just knew it as the sea monster. With the Sentinel at twenty, that meant she must surely be much older than thirty, even if she didn't look it. Her eyes appeared bright enough to light fire, but they were unreadable, as though a wall had been built to conceal a thousand thoughts.

But whenever Orin was around Commander Forge, he couldn't help the cold prickles of nerves that ran the length of his body. She was always calm and generally smiled at him, but the other servers had warned that she had a ruthless streak. Commander Forge liked things done a certain way, her way, and there was no room for error. But he guessed she had to be like that, because things in Ironhold ran like clockwork. She smiled. "You may go about your morning chores."

He gave a respectful nod and hurried past her to the cutlery drawers.

Forge sat at the table watching while he laid the table for the engineers who would soon arrive. "Your grandmother was Merina Crowfall, I believe?" she said suddenly.

"Yes, Commander." His stomach tightened. She never had showed any personal interest in him before.

"She showed a lot of promise as an engineer, or so I remember, but she was a rebellious soul. It's like the food that grows in our cultivation towers. Occasionally, the growers produce something that falls outside the high standards that Ironhold demands. A product may be irregular in some way.

Do you understand?"

He wasn't sure that he did, but he nodded. Was she calling Grandma irregular? It was hard to tell from her tone if she meant this as a good or bad thing.

"I'm sure you know the story of your ancestor Eros Crowfall, famous for ridding the city of its crow problem."

"Yes, Commander."

"It must've hurt your family to lose its standing on Ironhold after what your grandmother did. But you will always have that Eros Crowfall heritage, and for that reason I would like to see you progress beyond life as a server. Maybe even to a position in the Engineerium."

He nodded keenly, thinking how his parents would dearly wish that, but inside his guts twisted because he'd much rather spend his time climbing, and with plants.

"It's down to us to maintain the standards, to live by the rules. Do you see what I'm saying, Orin? We need to behave in a certain way to thrive, working together for the greater good. Rational, ordered choices are what makes things work. It keeps the technological evolution in place."

His cheeks filled with heat at the thought of how he'd been sneaking around the Engineerium. He'd tried not to do it too often, and he now wondered if he should change his plan to visit the conservatory after work that evening.

But last time at the Eard, he'd discovered a strange rotten patch on the roots. What if the Core hadn't discovered it yet? This morning he'd brought along one of his home-made plant tonics, in the hopes that it could help the Eard. But now he wondered if he should wait a day or two, just in case ... but he was excited to try his tonic, and in his experience, the longer you left a plant's problem, the worse it could get.

"Here, open the bottom drawer of the food supplies. There are some misshapen fruits and vegetables. Take them when you leave. Much as they don't meet the standards required for the quota, nothing can be wasted on Ironhold."

Orin opened the door and, alongside the usual breakfast supplies, there was a basket with a double carrot, undersized strawberries and a bent leek. The strawberries made his mouth water. Mum said he'd eaten them, before West Tip, and so many times he'd imagined the flavour as he served them to the engineers. "But we've had our quota for the week," he said guiltily.

She put a finger to her lips and smiled. "Our secret."

Later that day, rather than heading straight home after evening service at the Engineerium, Orin found himself sneaking into one of the passageways. The pull to try his tonic was too great.

When the footsteps of engineers leaving for the day had faded, and he was sure no one was in the atrium, he climbed down into the maze of pipes surrounding the conservatory, found the gap above the water pipe leading in, and squeezed through.

The air inside was warm and humid.

"It's me," he whispered, feeling a bit daft, because it wasn't like the Eard could talk back. Everything was still, then a small, white flower blossomed on a stem close to his fingers. It was strange, but he wondered if it was the Eard trying to communicate with him. This sort of thing happened every now and then since he'd been visiting, and although it had taken him by surprise at first, he was getting used to it. He stepped carefully through the plants towards the centre. There was no earth to walk on as such: instead, the "ground" was composed of thousands of twisted roots, so he had to tread carefully. In the centre of the conservatory the roots opened out and it was possible to peer down below the ground. When he'd first dared to come here, he'd been amazed to find a beautiful cavern of twisted stems and lights.

He smiled to himself and climbed down. This was the place he loved most, the place where all trace of Ironhold melted away.

As he moved through the roots, he spotted a glowing power pod – just like the one he'd used to fix Cody – growing not far below, a small globe the size of a child's fist that fizzled with silvery electric light. But when he climbed deeper into the Eard, he caught sight of someone below.

Every muscle in his body tensed.

Squinting into the dim light, Orin recognized the figure. It was Commander Forge!

Not knowing what to do, he froze. Forge reached her hands towards the roots. A strange pulsing white light began shining in the roots around her, like ripples of electricity. Beautiful aqua and silver specks of light danced within, as though the roots were veins filled with magical blood. As they glimmered, they began to flow in a common direction towards the commander, being drawn to her palms.

A strange yearning came over Orin, an urge to reach out and touch this spellbinding light, to be part of it. He resisted the feeling, but took a step down to the root below to see more clearly.

Faster, the silver slithers of light flowed towards Forge. Orin's heart twisted with jealousy as he thought how wonderful it must feel to be Commander Forge, to have been chosen as custodian and to have this connection with this magical creature. The roots beneath Forge's hands pooled with bright blue-white light, shining on Ironhold's leader as though she'd become a celestial star. What *was* this strange light?

That was the moment when Forge pulled a large, spear-like iron-and-glass implement from the long sleeve of her robe. She lifted it above her head.

Time seemed to pause.

Then, with furious speed, she plunged the spear into the root. The suddenness of her violence made Orin's stomach lurch, and he clamped a hand to his mouth to stifle a gasp. Everything around him tensed as though it had turned to concrete: his muscles, the roots, the very air. An uncomfortable, wheezy scream filled the underground cavern.

And then luminous silver liquid was flowing into the spear from the root, filling the glass vessel within. What was Forge doing? Now the light inside the roots turned an angry purple, and black veins spread out from the spear tip, the area around it becoming dead and hard, like a rapid frost. The leaves around Orin stiffened, their colour dulled, and he felt through his hands that the temperature of the roots he clutched was dropping. Was it the Eard shaking, or was it he himself – or both? Whatever was going on, Orin knew that he shouldn't be here. He should go, right now.

There was a hiss of air as Forge removed the spear, then she took what appeared to be a couple of small vials from her pocket and placed them on the ground. She upended the spear, unscrewed the glass vessel containing the silver liquid, and carefully poured the substance into the vials.

And then she looked up.

CHAPTER 5

It was eerily quiet as Orin ran down the steps to the under-rail. As soon as Commander Forge had looked in his direction, he'd sunk into the leaves, then hurriedly scrambled back up.

Panic coursed through him. What if she'd seen him? No, he told himself, he had hidden himself well enough and managed to scurry his way out by weaving through the vines undetected. But worse than the thought of being seen was wondering what she'd been doing to the Eard! It looked as if she had *hurt* it. But that couldn't be the case, could it? Maybe it was something else. He couldn't be entirely sure.

By the time Orin reached West Tip, the sun had almost set and his spinning thoughts had calmed somewhat. No one had followed him, there had been no sirens or alarms – he hadn't been spotted. He was safe, for the time being. He didn't trust himself to keep his secrets if he went home, so he went to the southern point clifftop to clear his head instead.

The ferocity of Forge's actions stayed with Orin in an uncomfortable tightness in his stomach. It was how the Eard had reacted too: the fear it seemed to feel. But Orin was sure that Commander Forge, as their great leader and Custodian of the Eard, must have been doing it for good reasons, even if he didn't understand them. His mind buzzed with questions.

"There you are." Cody fluttered to land beside him. "It was getting late. I thought I'd find you here."

Relief flooded him to see Cody's friendly face. She knew him so well. "You won't believe what I saw." He recounted what had happened.

Cody's wing blades gave an uncomfortable shudder. "What did she do with the liquid she collected?"

"I didn't get a chance to see. That's when she looked up."

"And you're sure she didn't see you?"

"I'm pretty sure."

"Perhaps you should stop sneaking around."

Of course she was right, but Orin was already thinking about when he'd have the next opportunity to take another look. The Eard had looked to be in pain, and no matter how much of a bad idea it was, he felt compelled to check on it.

In the distance, dark clouds loomed on the horizon. Orin squinted to see which direction they were moving. He hoped another storm wasn't coming.

Something glinted and rose from the ocean, arching over the waves, serpentine in its body shape. A cold shard of ice ran the length of Orin's spine: it was the mechanical sea monster. Sightings were rare, as the beast usually stayed at the place where the seas met, known as the Divide, a point out at sea where the brown-green sediments from the north met the clearer blue water from the south and caused a natural line. The sea monster protected Ironhold from potential invaders. But it worked both ways: much as it kept people out, it made it impossible for Ironhold inhabitants to leave.

It had killed Orin's grandma.

Grandma had been a born adventurer, and in her

younger years she had filled her book with tales and jottings of islands. Then the monster, this Sentinel, was introduced, and the next time she ventured out into the sea, it was her last ever trip. Orin's grandma's reckless curiosity had brought disgrace on the family, and it was the reason they'd been moved to West Tip.

Orin jabbed his finger at the horizon. "There, Cody! Do you see the monster?"

"My eyes are far superior to your human ones. Of course I can."

"I've never seen it so close." The metal creature disappeared beneath the waves. Orin drew in a lungful of chill, salty air. "Do you ever wonder what life is like out there? Far away?"

"I'm a robot, we're not meant to wonder," she said, with a twinkle in her eye. "But, yes, I do."

"You're no ordinary robot."

"Affirmative."

Orin rolled his eyes.

They were about to head home when, a short distance from the north side of the island, the mechanical sea monster rose again, its enormous tubular steel body undulating, hooked dorsal fins slicing through the water. Its great electric eye glinted and there was the sound of metal grating against metal. Orin's breath caught as the sight of it filled him with fear. "What's it doing so close?"

"Possibly coming in for maintenance," Cody suggested.

The monster was heading towards the north of the island, where the robot factories were, so Orin thought Cody was probably right.

"Come on. Let's get back home."

The next morning, Orin dressed for work as if nothing had changed. He knew that if Forge had really spotted him, he would have been hauled in already, but he still couldn't help worrying.

"You're a jumping jack of a thing this morning," Cody remarked. "You're not entirely convinced she didn't see you, are you?"

"I'm ninety-nine point nine per cent sure she didn't." Well, that was what he was telling himself as he tried to ignore the butterflies about seeing Commander Forge again.

"I'll come with you and hang out with the fixies outside until you finish. The juniper is fixing up fine, and I could do with a change of scene."

Orin was glad she'd offered. Even if she couldn't come inside the Engineerium, Orin liked having his friend close. "Thanks, Cody."

When he arrived at work, Orin kept his head down and went about his job. From the glass lift, he caught glimpses of Cody, who had joined some other fixies repairing a crack in one of the towers opposite the Engineerium. To everyone else Cody blended in perfectly with the other robots, but Orin was familiar with the nuances in her movements, like the slight inquisitive tilt to her head and the way she gave her wings a little shiver when she concentrated.

When Commander Forge entered the room, Orin waited nervously at the edge with the ten other servers. Usually, it was just him serving breakfast, while the others were in the kitchens doing prep or serving elsewhere, but not today; a big meeting of the Core had been called.

"Good morning," she said to no one in particular, and went to sit down at the table. There was something even more glowing and radiant about her today, as though she had just come back from a brisk walk outside, and her voice was light and breezy. Her smile and the fact that she didn't seem at all interested in him put Orin at ease. Shoulders relaxing, he let out a soft breath of relief. He was now certain she hadn't seen him last night.

The remaining nine Core engineers began entering the room and joining Commander Forge at the table. They were all dressed in their black trousers, white shirts and scarlet capes, pinned at the chest with the metal symbol of Ironhold. Orin knew them all by name now: Ferreira Ore with long shiny hair and suspicious scowl; Silver Blecher with his smooth dark skin and long limbs, designer of the Ironhold's weather protection; Senga and Artemas Anvil, white haired twins, mathematical geniuses who could say so much with a glance; Eli Ward, the oldest of the group, his face in a permanent frown; Yarik Whitesmith, short and always swift in his movements; Denira Goldsmith, who oversaw the cultivation towers and always sat to the right of Vida Forge; Thetus Black with his sleek smooth hair, also a whizz with transport design such as the recent hover bike; and Ami Greenspan, the original fixie designer.

Orin was soon busily adding to the platters of

fruit and warm bread, and refilling cups with the finest juice from the cultivation towers as though it were water. One of the older servers placed a platter of the rare food known as *chocolate* on the table, and the scent made his stomach groan longingly.

The Core engineers chatted excitedly with one another in low tones. As Orin poured juice and replenished bowls, he heard enticing words such as *everlasting, miracle* and *for ever,* but then the engineers would catch his eye and stop talking until he moved on to top up the next glass. Something was going on.

He was refilling sweet berry juice into Commander Forge's cup when she announced that the servers were dismissed from duty until lunch.

Orin paused, wondering if he should clear the plates first.

Forge smiled, seeing his confusion. "Don't worry about them for today."

As he left the room, a feeling in the pit of his stomach tugged as though trying to pull him back. Commander Forge had clearly sent the servers away so that the Core could have a private discussion. Orin found his feet taking him away from the lift and down the stairs towards the maintenance cupboard on the floor below. The certainty that something was going on had lodged itself inside of him, and the hushed snippets he had heard at breakfast, combined with what he'd seen last night, meant he couldn't help himself.

After a swift look over his shoulder, Orin sneaked into the cupboard, moved aside a box, lifted the vent flap and crawled inside, turning left to take himself beneath room 505. He crawled, then crossed into the shaft that took the food up from the kitchens next door to the cupboard. He checked there were no trays in the shaft and, silently as breath, climbed upwards using the pulley ropes to heave himself up. When he was up a level, he crept out of the shaft and into the larder cupboard of room 505. Commander Forge was addressing the room.

" . . . timing is of the essence . . . life-light. . ."

Orin's thoughts fizzled like electricity. *What was life-light?* But even as the question entered his mind, he remembered the dance of silver and aqua light last night. Straining to hear, he leant further towards the larder door.

"As you know, large areas of the island are

increasingly unstable. The fixies are managing to mend any affected buildings before the people notice. However, the latest reports show that, in short, the Eard is failing, and if we continue along this track, Ironhold won't survive. In order for us to persist, we must . . . expand our horizons."

Orin stomach twisted. *Ironhold was failing?* That didn't sound good, to put it mildly. But why? And what did she mean by expanding their horizons?

Forge's footsteps echoed around the room. "Storm frequency is increasing, our crops aren't doing well, buildings are falling into the sea, our summers are hotter and hotter, the winters colder, air pollution is rising, and I believe it all to be directly linked to the Eard. We work the island hard in order to thrive, but our harvesting of life-light is accelerating the side effects beyond what we can control."

Further along between the larder doors, a string-thin slither of light seeped inside. Orin crept towards it, then pressed his eye to the gap.

Commander Forge placed a tiny decorative vial in front of each of the Core engineers. "I have gifts for you all."

A silvery glow shone through the patterned glass

of the vials. There was something wild and feverish about the way the engineers stared at them, as though they held the last scraps of food on Ironhold.

"Given what I have told you, you might think that the only way forward is to stop taking the life-light. But, where would any of us be if we didn't push the boundaries of technological evolution? I propose that we simply need to cultivate a newer, purer source. So before you drink, I have news. As you know, Denira has been travelling beyond the borders, seeking potential islands for us to occupy."

Orin tried to make sense of what he was hearing, but the ideas were too big, too all-encompassing: Ironhold breaking down, failing? Moving to a new island? His whole world would change completely.

"How will we transport the people?" asked one of the Core, whom Orin recognized as Thetus Black.

"Dear Thetus, isn't it obvious? The supply of life-light is for the chosen few only: you, the ten highest-order engineers in the city. The Core. I am sharing it with you now, as promised. But we don't need the rest of Ironhold weighing us down. How would the inhabitants of West Tip, or the common workers, help us form a society we're proud of?

It's perfectly rational that the Core survive. I have found a way to a life everlasting, the next step in technological and human evolution, and there is only enough for the privileged few. The best few. Everyone in Ironhold has their role, but now it is time for them to play the ultimate part. Sacrifice for the good of the future way."

Fear reached into Orin's heart and gripped it tight. Forge spoke as if it was a perfectly acceptable next step in the evolution of Ironhold, but nothing about it sounded rational to him. If he was hearing correctly, the Core only planned to save themselves. They had some sort of life-extending force, something that only the Eard could provide. Surely it was in the vials before each of the Core, the same small glass bottles of silvery liquid he'd seen Commander Forge with at the Eard. This liquid, or "life-light" as she'd called it, seemed to be the key to eternal life, but, if he'd understood correctly, taking it had consequences and was killing their island.

"Are you saying we start a new life, and we don't need the rest of the people of Ironhold? It will be just the ten of us?" said another of the Core hesitantly. They were out of view but Orin thought it was the voice of Ami Greenspan.

"With the life-light there is no need for others. Not for numerous engineers, growers, maintenance, researchers or even servers. If there are too many, it will jeopardize resources. All we need is a new Eard and ourselves; then we will live a life eternal, never wanting for anything. With no one else to worry about, imagine the greatness we could achieve? You are in the Core for one reason: you are the greatest minds in Ironhold." Forge looked around the room at each of the Core, eyes shining brighter than ever. "Although, if you feel your role lies elsewhere, if you are not strong enough to endure, I invite you to speak now and relinquish your space."

The next few moments weighed heavily, and Orin concentrated on staying perfectly still, while inside of him a storm of confused thoughts raged. Denira Goldsmith, face hard as granite, stared admiringly at Forge; there was no way she would go against her. The Anvil twins exchanged a secret glance and soft grin. Silver Blecher frowned hard. Eli Ward, the oldest of the Core, moved back and forward in his chair, Orin decided in more of an excited than agitated way, his usual pallid skin looking flushed.

Soundlessly, Orin adjusted his stance to try and see the others. Surely one was going to declare that this was preposterous, madness, and that their duty was to the people of Ironhold? Silver Blecher came into view, his frown deep. His hands clenched. His lips parted. Then shut. Yarik Goldsmith had his back to Orin, but his feet were fidgeting beneath the table. Again nothing.

Forge smiled. "Then we shall drink a toast, to the next advancement of humankind. To the new way. A life eternal."

Orin pressed his eye as close as he could to the gap as Commander Forge unstoppered her vial and drank. He watched in amazement as the lines around her eyes faded and her skin seemed to brighten a tone and become more dewy, smooth and glowing.

So this was why she appeared so ageless!

The other nine engineers followed and the same happened to them. One, Ami Greenspan, even lost the flecks of grey in her hair as it turned a glossy dark brown.

Orin noticed that Silver Blecher hadn't drunk his yet. "Can't we simply stay here, keep repairing the buildings and fortifying the cliffs? We all have families here. How can we just abandon them?"

Commander Forge stood before him. "My dear Silver, if there was a way, I would make it happen. The years of extraction have taken their toll on the Eard. It is unable to keep up with our demand. In short, it is almost spent, and it is a matter of time before it dies and the island falls to the sea. Yes, it may take several years, but why prolong the inevitable? We need a more youthful supply. The next stage of technological advancement does not lie in the structures of Ironhold ... it lies in its ideas. The advancement comes from within each of us here. We are the next stage in its evolution. But a few extras to help with lesser tasks may be useful." She frowned in thought, then lifted the vial to his lips. "I will allow close family of my choice, no negotiation. They won't be informed until the day. Now, drink."

Orin could hardly believe what he was hearing. Wasn't even *one* of these engineers going to speak up for the thousands of people living in Ironhold?

"If the island collapses, where will they go?" asked an engineer just out of Orin's sight.

"It will no longer be our concern. It is natural

for the strongest brains to survive, the only rational course of action for the future. Those clouded by emotion will never see the true greatness that can be achieved." Thetus Black and Eli Ward nodded thoughtfully. "You could give up your place, Ferreira? If you believe you are not worthy?"

"Oh, no, I was just curious of the logistics. After all, they have boats. We can't be expected to do everything for them."

Murmurs of agreement echoed around the table. She had every single one of them on board.

Orin felt another surge of outrage. These were the island leaders; they were meant to look after the people! He wanted to shake them, make them realize what they were saying, what this would mean for so many people. How could they abandon them like they were nothing?

"Good. Then as we are all on board, I'm pleased to announce that we have found an uninhabited island to the east which looks suitable for planting a new Eard. Ironhold's Eard seems to have stopped producing seed pods, but I have taken the last few."

Gasps of excitement rippled around the table. Forge held the palm-sized pod. It was identical to the pod that Orin had used as a power source for Cody.

"I propose we immediately begin preparations for the journey, as it won't be long before the Eard will have regenerated its life-light to satisfactory levels for us to take one final supply."

"Commander, am I right in saying that will be the last of the Eard of Ironhold?" asked Yarik Whitesmith.

"You are correct, Yarik. It is inevitable that the island will disintegrate. It has served its purpose." The matter-of-factness in her tone was chilling. "So it is agreed. Ten days from now, we leave."

The shock of her words jolted Orin. Ten days! He sucked in a loud gasp of air and immediately realized his mistake. He froze as the voices outside fell silent.

The door whipped open.

Orin's eyes locked with Commander Forge's.

CHAPTER 6

Orin scuttled back towards the shaft. Lunging inside, Commander Forge grabbed his shirt and a button came away in her hand as he dropped out of the back end of the larder and into the kitchen shaft. He crashed and clanged against the walls as he fell down one storey and landed with a painful *thud* on the shaft's floor below, metal clanging and echoing through the building.

His shoulder burned horribly, and he thought he'd twisted his ankle, but there was no time to think about that now. He had to get away. Forcing himself on hands and knees, he hurried along the vent back towards the maintenance cupboard. As he pushed open the vent, the metallic pound of robot guards charging sounded down the stairs.

Heart in his throat, he dived out of the wall vent, tumbled through the cupboard doors and landed a short distance from the lift. The shadows of the guards appeared on the wall as he scrambled to his feet, jabbed the button and begged for it to come. In a moment it was there, and as the robot guards ran towards him, the doors slid shut and he was shooting down to the bottom floor.

Alarms sounded as he rushed across the atrium. Engineers and other workers looked around, confused. He pushed through them towards the door. The pounding sound of metal footsteps rang in his ears as he ran. The main door was open, as an engineer had just walked through into the building. Someone called out, "Stop him!" If he didn't make it outside, that would be it. With only a small gap left, he twisted his body sideways and slipped through just in time. The glass door sucked closed behind him, and he glanced over his shoulder to see a guard sliding to a halt, inches away on the other side.

What now? He ran across the square towards the under-rail, calling out for Cody, people staring as he yelled. If what he'd heard was true, then there was no future for his family – or anyone here. His parents' and Grandpa's friends, the people he went to school with – what would happen to all of them if they were left alone on an island that was crumbling into the sea?

It was all too big and awful to consider.

He'd focus on Mum and Dad and Grandpa for now. There was nothing he could do for Ironhold, but he could warn his family. Grandma's book might help them find a safe place somewhere beyond the horizon. He'd get home, grab some supplies, get everyone into a boat, and they could leave before Orin was caught and imprisoned – or worse – for what he'd heard.

He jumped as Cody flew up beside him. "What in all pumping pistons has got into you? What's going on at the Engineerium?"

Hurriedly he glanced behind. The Engineerium's main door was open again and several robot guards were heading for him.

Breathless, he managed, "Get away ... now ... under-rail."

Seeing his distress, she nodded, and they hurried down to the platform. Orin gave a silent plea that an under-rail train would be there, but to no avail. The platform was empty. Putting his hands on his knees, he gasped and looked back to the moving stairs. Maybe they'd lost them. But then the clanking feet of a guard appeared and his heart sank. A rush of warm wind enveloped the platform and Cody grabbed his hand. "We need to get as far along as we can."

And then, to his relief, a train whooshed into view, the doors slid open and they jumped on. But the robot guard was suddenly behind them on the platform. It sprang for Orin. Quick as a blink, Cody flipped back a thumb, clicked her fingers and lit an electrical spark. She jabbed it at the guard. Electrical fizzles rippled where she'd poked the guard, and it stumbled away from the under-train.

After an excruciating moment, there was a bleep and the door shut. The train sped off and the guard was left on the platform.

The carriage was empty. Slumping into a seat, Orin caught his breath. "That was a neat move. Thanks."

"You've got some pretty big explaining to do," said Cody.

*

By the time they reached West Tip, Orin had told Cody everything. When they emerged, a fog had settled on the streets of West Tip and Orin could see only a short distance in every direction. "I'll find Mum and Dad. You go and explain to Grandpa, and we'll all leave." Although where they would go, he hadn't worked out yet. He just hoped the islands in Grandma's book turned out to be real. Or maybe they could find the one that Denira had found.

"Your grandpa isn't aware I talk. Don't you think he'll find it a bit strange?"

"Probably, but—"

"—And suppose we get a boat and leave straight away. What about the sea monster?"

Tears threatened with the frustration and churning confusion Orin felt. "I don't know!" he snapped, stopping dead in the alley. Everything was out of control and impossible.

Cody fluttered and hovered so that her large black eyes were level with Orin's; her antennae were alert. She grabbed his face between her metal hands. "We'll take whatever tools we can find, and we'll make a weapon, that's what. But we must act quick—"

Her words jolted. Metallic footsteps could be heard in the adjacent alley, the one between them and home. Dread reached into Orin's chest and grasped his heart. The guards had caught up. They wouldn't make it.

Cody put a finger to her lips, then whispered: "If we get to the cliff edge, we can climb in your window and warn Grandpa."

As they turned, a guard emerged from the fog facing them. Instinctively, they ran in the other direction, but another guard appeared, blocking their way.

"Keep running!" shouted Cody.

"What?" he screeched. He was meant to keep running at the guard?

"Trust me!"

Just before they reached him, Cody shouted, "Jump!"

As Orin leapt, the motors of Cody's wings switched to full power, she grabbed the back of his shirt, and they rose into the air and over the guard. They landed by the entrance to the small alley which led to the south-west beach. If they could get far enough along this way before the guards passed, the fog would swallow them up and the guards might think they'd carried on along the main alley.

Orin ran down the cliff steps to the small beach. It was a long, treacherous route, but there was no time for careful stepping. As long as they got away from the guards pursuing them, they could hide and wait it out until it was safe to get a message home. Orin knew a small cave at the end of the beach where they could hide for a while.

At the bottom, Orin looked up and tried to catch his breath again. There was no guard in pursuit.

Cody fluttered next to him. "Are you thinking the cave?"

Orin nodded. "We'll wait there until it's dark."

But Orin had forgotten about the route that cut into the south-west beach from the other side. Air blasted him as something shot towards them, whooshing to a halt a stone's throw away in their path: a hover bike.

Riding it was Commander Forge.

"Orin Crowfall! You're quite the unexpected thorn in the patch!"

"Commander Forge!" Orin squeaked in shock, looking around for the best escape. There was no way he would make it back up the steps. After all the exertion, his muscles felt like water. Besides, there would still be guards at the top. Next to him, the rickety wooden jetty used to have dozens of boats moored to it, but the cliff above had eroded too much and the boats had been moved on, to avoid being smashed from falling chunks.

"Any ideas, oh, bright human brain?" said Cody, her voice cracking.

"I was hoping you'd compute a way out of this."

Slowly they backed up the jetty as Commander Forge left the hover bike and took step after step towards them.

"Well, there is one option." Orin spotted a seemingly forgotten old boat bobbing in the soft roll of the tide, still tied alongside the jetty.

Commander Forge darted towards them.

"Now!" Orin shouted and, unhooking the rope from the jetty, he launched himself at the boat. As he landed with a *thud*, Orin saw Cody, flying alongside, being wrenched backwards. For a heart-stopping moment Orin realized Commander Forge had caught her. There was no way he was leaving her. In one swift motion, he sprang up and managed to grab Cody's hand, pulling with all his might. He heard a strange *pop* of metal and felt something give, before Cody clattered into the boat next to him. Lightning quick, Orin pushed away from the jetty with his feet so that the boat rushed out of Forge's reach and into the sea.

As Orin fumbled for the oars, he saw something metal in Commander Forge's hands. He looked at Cody in confusion. "Your wings!"

Cody sat shocked and shivering in the boat, but there was no going back to the jetty.

Guards appeared beside Commander Forge, staring out, perplexed. But the steely gaze of the commander was unwavering. He saw a wry grin cross her lips. She knew they were stuck.

Orin rowed until his arm muscles burned and Ironhold was a dark, blurry shape in the mist. The boat juddered and Orin realized Cody was shaking . . . and that he was too. "Are you all right?"

Cody nodded. "I know I'm a robot and things aren't meant to hurt, but. . ."

The day was overcast, and sea mist smudged the horizon in all directions.

"I'm so sorry. We can get you new ones."

Cody laughed in a panicked way. "Orin, we're in a boat, in the middle of the sea, with a bunch of Ironhold guards ready to arrest us the moment we return, and you're worried about replacing my wings."

"We need to get back to warn Mum, Dad and Grandpa. . ."

Cody stayed silent.

"What?" he said.

"Well, if everything you heard is true, then what about everybody else on Ironhold?"

"Cody, I'm not some Engineerium whizz with all the answers, or the power to do anything. I don't know."

"No, you're just Orin from West Tip," she said with not a little sarcasm. "And you feel out of your depth."

"There's no need to get ratty with me. It's not my fault."

Waves slapped the sides of the boat and they lolled from side to side. If he hadn't spied on the meeting, he wouldn't be in this position right now: Cody wouldn't have lost her wings, he would be on his way to school as normal. . . But he also wouldn't know what Forge was planning. At least now he had a chance to do something – even if he hadn't quite yet worked out what, or how.

He folded his arms and the warmth of exertion began to fade, the cold seeping into his skin. Suddenly he realized the mist had become thicker and he could hardly see Ironhold any more. Soon they were enveloped by thick grey cloud. The boat swayed more violently. "Where's Ironhold? Can you still see it?"

"I have powerful vision, but I can't *actually* see through things, and my sonar systems are being scrambled by high levels of electrical activity in the atmosphere." Cody sidled up close to Orin as they both strained to make out any shapes in the impenetrable grey.

Then lightning pulsed through the fog.

Orin swallowed hard. "I think our situation is about to get worse."

A storm was coming.

CHAPTER 7

Orin and Cody rowed blindly in what they hoped was the direction of Ironhold. With the storm approaching, they had no choice but to return.

"At least with the storm it'll be easier to avoid the guards. It might be a good thing. Let's get as close as we can and then find somewhere on the island to hide," Orin said, trying to keep the doubt and fear from his voice. The idea of being stuck in the middle of the ocean during a storm terrified him. No one could survive that.

Cody stayed silent and they carried on rowing. The fog cleared a little and Orin began to feel hopeful that Ironhold would appear.

But it didn't.

A loud *bang* tilted the boat violently, throwing Orin and Cody forward.

When he pulled himself up and looked around, Orin saw a flash in the water. There was something in the sea.

"Cody ... I think..." Had they gone too far? Surely they couldn't have come *this* far?

With a surge of fear, he saw something a little way from the boat: the sea changed colour. There was a stripe of white across the surface and then slightly paler water beyond. The borders of Ironhold's territorial waters, where the seas met.

"We're at the Divide," he said in hushed terror.

Another flash sparked in the water. Something huge and metallic undulated beneath the water a short distance from them. A creeping dread gripped him: there was no mistaking the menacing coils that snaked through the waves. "I think it's ... the mechanical sea monster."

If they crossed the line, the sea monster would attack for sure. The currents must have carried them in the wrong direction – many ironspans away from Ironhold. How had they got so far without realizing?

He looked up at the ever-darkening clouds. "Quick – row in the other direction!"

They turned the boat and rowed hard, but the current was too strong and they were still heading the wrong way. They were being sucked towards the mechanical sea monster. Lightning lit the sky, and Orin counted: one rivet, two rivets, three rivets...

Thunder snarled in the distance. "Ten rivets."

Cody quivered. Lightning flashed again, and thunder growled almost simultaneously.

Panic started to seize Orin. The first drops of rain splashed on the wooden seat. The boat swayed heftily in the wind and waves, and within moments the sky opened with a deluge of rainfall. Then, just as suddenly, impenetrable cloud, darker than the mist, swamped them again, as if someone had drawn a curtain around the boat.

Waves rolled in queasy rhythms, gaining momentum. "At least the choppy waters might keep the sea monster away," Orin called to Cody, doing his best to stay calm.

Jagged blades of lightning stabbed the sea. Cody looked at him with frightened, wide eyes. If the lightning struck any closer it could burn them to charcoal. "We need to get away from the storm, Cody. Row!"

The storm spun them round and Orin knew they were fighting a losing battle. "It's no use! Get the oars in and hold on."

When the storm cleared, Orin guardedly untensed his body and released Cody. He had spent several centidays curled up in a ball, shivering and soaking, huddling over her, trying to keep her dry. It had been the only thing he could do. "Are you all right?"

She nodded. "I feel like every cog and nut in my body is rattling, but I'm alive. You?"

"Same."

Yanking himself into action, Orin looked around for the mechanical sea monster. It had felt as though they had travelled hundreds of ironspans, the storm waves chewing and spitting them out again. There was no sign of the creature here, or the meeting line in the seas.

And no sign of Ironhold.

He tried to push away the thought that they were

lost at sea, many ironspans from home, without equipment, food or water, but it was like attempting to stop an open hydro-gate. And he tried even harder to push away the bleak thought that he might never see his family again.

Those thoughts wouldn't help him now. The clouds parted a little and sun fought its way through. He set himself a focus. "Cody, look, the sun is there, so that," he said, pointing to his right, "must be north. We need to row that way."

Glancing over the side of the boat, the water was clear as a fine jewel. Coral was visible in the shallower waters. A shoal of small silver fish flittered past.

The water only seemed about a person deep in places, Orin guessed. Perhaps he could dive and catch a fish with a spear, like he did off the cliffs of West Tip. Except he had no spear.

And then a glint below the surface made his heart turn to iron. Was it the mechanical sea monster?

No, this thing wasn't moving.

"What, in all of Ironhold, is that?" Cody climbed on the boat edge and peered over as they drifted above the huge silvery disc shape. There were etchings and patterns on it.

"Just like in Grandma's book," Orin breathed, looking at Cody. "You remember, the myths about creatures coming from above thousands of years ago. This could be one of their sky-vehicles from the stars!" Despite the peril of their situation, Orin's chest fizzled with possibility. It was incredible to see something so out of place in the sea. Something so seemingly impossible right in front of him. There was so much out here to discover.

Grandpa's face swam in Orin's mind's eye, and he pictured him sitting by the fire in his colourful armchair. Orin's heart churned with a mixture of longing to explore while also aching for home.

The sun sank lower, the air became sharp, and without any clue where they were, Orin kept his thoughts on the movement of his oar to keep himself from falling into despair.

Cody blinked her great wide eyes and they rowed on in silence until night deepened around them and blue moonlight danced on the waves and the sky above was filled with stars.

*

Orin suddenly leapt up. "We did it! It's Ironhold!

81

Cody, look. We're home!"

Although it was hard to see in the indigo of the night, they were indeed approaching an island, and it had tall structures rising high.

But Cody looked wary: at night, the spires of Ironhold glowed magnificently, but there were no lights visible on the island ahead of them. Had something happened?

"No, Orin, the shapes are all wrong."

The hope inside him turned to a concrete ball. "What is this place?" Orin could see now that it clearly wasn't Ironhold. Great arcs of rock criss-crossed out of the water around the island, as though they had once been part of a whole but had been gradually eroded over thousands of years until only the strongest struts survived. There was nothing like this in the waters around Ironhold.

What would happen to them out here? How long could they last? Hunger hollowed his belly, but much worse was the unbearable thirst he was starting to feel. He clamped his dry lips and took a long breath through his nose.

"Hey, we can wait until the sun comes up again and use it to navigate back. It'll be all right." Cody tried to smile, but even she couldn't mask that she felt as worried as him.

Then, behind them, they heard a splash. They spun around and something shot through the water towards them. It spiralled around and then a large metallic serpent head the size of their boat punched through the surface and launched into the air above them, followed by a huge cylindrical body. It was the mechanical sea monster! The water lurched their boat upwards and they found themselves looking up at cold, glowing eye receptors, and a mouth of steel dagger teeth. It curled above them, dorsal spines cutting the air, then landed with a splash behind them, its great long body and tail slicing inches from them and back beneath the water. The boat tilted almost on its side and they grabbed for anything they could in order to not be plunged into the sea.

As the boat calmed, Orin frantically scanned the ocean for the monster. He spotted a dark shape not far away, turning in the water.

"It's going to come back!" His voice was hoarse and scared. Cody tapped him wildly on the shoulder and pointed a moonlit hand at the arcs of rock.

"We could hide in there if we're careful!"

"Yes! Good thinking!"

Orin and Cody grasped the oars.

"Pull!" Orin yelled.

Before they could navigate a path, the boat took another impact from the sea monster. As Orin tried to stop himself falling out of the boat, the oars flew from his hand into the ocean. The boat surged and tilted. "It's pushing us into the rocks!"

They flew and bumped over the waves. Orin's screams felt like someone else's, and Cody was yelling and bouncing up and down like a loose bearing. Lunging forward, Orin managed to grab Cody's arm just as the back of the boat tilted into the sea waves and the front lifted.

The moonlit jagged rocks came at them like lightning.

With a bone-wrenching *crack*, Orin was hurled from the boat, smacking into the rocks and then into the sea. The churning chaos of water was all around, biting cold, rolling his body like a fabric toy. He fought desperately not to gasp for oxygen, then caught a flicker of metal as the mechanical sea monster bulleted towards him, and he cried out, inhaling acrid salt water. A burning sear exploded in his thigh. The pain was so intense he thought he might pass out, but adrenaline stopped him. If he passed out, it would all be over, so he kicked and kicked towards a white dancing spot of light above, before breaking the surface.

Spluttering and retching, he grabbed for what looked like half the boat, missed it, then lurched beneath the waves once more. Images of his parents and grandfather flashed though his mind. They would never know what had happened to him. The sea monster zoomed inexorably towards him. Then, by blind luck, the roll of the current tumbled Orin out of its path, though not before the creature's head had caught the side of Orin's ribs with a dull *boom*. He plummeted through the dizzying trail of bubbles in its wake, down and down. It was the thought that Cody was somewhere needing help that made him thrust once more for the surface. He bashed into freezing hard rock and caught a glimmer above. Cody. Somehow he broke the surface and gulped for air as she pulled him on to a wrecked piece of the boat. Satisfied it had defeated its foe, the lights of the sea monster faded into the distance.

Orin hung on to the wreckage like it was the last

piece of land in the world and they stayed together, carried by the tide, until the soft light of dawn was on the horizon. Then, exhausted, weak, and in agony with his leg, Orin gave in to unconsciousness and the tides of the sea.

CHAPTER 8

The lapping of waves on a beach woke Orin. He blinked heavy eyes and saw Cody looking down at him. She grasped his shoulders and hauled him backwards. He tried to move, to help in some way, but everything was either numb or aching. Throbbing pain pulsed in his leg, his chest felt sore, and it was hard to breathe. He was so thirsty he wasn't sure he could speak. His clothes were heavy, drenched with seawater. Chilled to the bone, he shivered.

When he attempted to lift his head, it felt as though his muscles had been fused by lead. He strained to see through blurry eyes. In the distance he could just make out patches of mist and, between them, thick, green luscious growth, like he'd fallen into the gardens of the Engineerium. Except this definitely wasn't Ironhold because this was vast and wide, wild and overgrown, like nothing he'd ever seen at home. Where was he? A sudden wave of pain in his leg took all his energy and made him claw at the sand. They were fine grains, similar to those of the small south beach of Ironhold. Perhaps, if he imagined really hard, he could be back there, lying on the beach, making sand fixie wings with his arms. Back home, where every sinew of him didn't hurt. Back with Mum, Dad and Grandpa.

Something tapped his face, hard.

It was Cody. "Orin, we survived."

Orin exhaled with a painful groan. He wanted to ask if she was all right but couldn't produce the words. His mouth was parched, his limbs were quivering and the cut on his thigh throbbed fiercely.

Orin glimpsed a shadow. They weren't alone.

Far away, faint voices drifted, muffled, as if they were underwater.

He heaved his head to the side and came face to face with a crustacean of sorts, and its eyes on stalks rose to meet his. It nipped him on the nose, and he yelped and thrust himself backwards as the startled creature scuttled away. He groaned as the sky above spun.

Soon, shadows bathed him, and a girl peered down with eyes as green as spring. The bottom half of her face was covered by a scarf or mask, and her hair was cloaked.

"He's alive!" she said.

Drops of water fell on his lips, but he was too exhausted to lift his head.

Something prodded him hard in the ribs where the sea monster had hit, and he cried out in pain. Fear seeped through his veins; what was going to happen to him on this strange island? The mechanical sea monster had been created to protect Ironhold from outsiders who meant them harm, and here he was, right in harm's way.

"Nara, stop! He's hardly in a position to be a threat." Orin felt reassured that this new voice didn't sound hostile.

"What's this *thing*?" said the first voice, sterner, more suspicious. That one must be Nara, he thought hazily, but his mind was too clouded and his vision too blurred to see properly.

He thought Cody said something, but her words were muffled by the rush of blood in his ears as another throb of pain stabbed his thigh.

"We'll need a bog myrtle. He's too heavy."

"Too heavy for what? Ferelith, you're not seriously considering—"

"We can't *leave* him like this."

"But to take him back to Heart Tree? Are you out of your mind? I'm not risking a punishment for anyone. Not even you. The rules are clear. Outsiders are to be turned away."

"But there hasn't been an outsider here in years. Besides, that rule was made for potential invaders. Look at the state of him! A wheatenhog has more muscles than him."

If Orin hadn't felt so desperately weak he would have objected, but instead he groaned what he hoped sounded like, *"Help."*

"Nara, he'll die if we don't take him home."

Die? No, he wouldn't. Orin tried to force himself into a sitting position. He had to explain what had happened. But his vision was closing as though he was disappearing down a long tunnel. He tried to latch on to the rhythmic rush of waves as he fought to breathe steadily.

"Fine, have it your way," said the snappy girl. "Why is it you find it so hard to listen?"

Then one of them made a strange low bawling sound that made Orin's chest judder. His eyelids were too leaden to look at what was going on. Shortly, there was shuffling, and strong hands lifted him under his armpits. He tried to say something about not leaving Cody, but his voice sounded distant and the world tilted and spun.

And then he was being carried on the back of something warm and mossy. There were moments of flitting between realms of consciousness to see pools of brown-green shade and light fading to twilight, before, finally, he submitted to the endless black tunnel.

When Orin woke, he was in a domed room, but it wasn't made of brick, or stone, or glass. Instead, twisted mossy vines shaped the ceiling and walls, as though he lay inside a cavity of tree roots. The air was warm and tranquil, and there was an earthy scent tinged with something like the fresh herbs that grew in the cultivation towers. He lay upon a bed made from woven seagrass, with a comfortable cotton mattress, his sheet soft and silken. This place was nothing like home. For a moment he lingered in an unearthly world of not knowing who or where he was, then a storm of memories swelled in his chest and he sat bolt upright. How long had he been here?

"Cody!" he cried out, but his voice was scratchy and hurt.

Scuttling from beneath his bed, Cody's huge eyes stared. "I've been trying to wake you—"

"Thank goodness. Are you all right? What time is it?"

"It's morning."

He breathed out in relief. The sea monster had attacked at night and then they'd washed up on the shore, and it seemed to still be daytime, so not much time had passed. "OK, so we still have nine days before the Core finish off the Eard and leave Ironhold. We need to get there as soon as possible. We should head back to the beach and salvage what's left of the boat." He had no plan for how to actually get back home, or what to do if he managed it, but he didn't have a hope of saving anyone if he stayed here.

"Orin, it's the morning *after* the day we arrived here. It's been three days since we left Ironhold."

Panic coursed through him. They'd lost so much time.

"You were sleeping, and that girl gave you something, then you slept more."

He remembered the girl from the beach with the bright green eyes.

"I tried to stop her," Cody continued, "but she's very persuasive and. . ."

Orin patted Cody's head. "I'm awake now." He looked around, wondering what these people would do to him when they returned. But Cody was there and there was something calm and natural about the room he was in. "Did anyone try to hurt you?"

She shook her head. "The girl seems kind," she said, as if reading his thoughts.

"Your joints sound creaky, what's wrong?"

"I've been rolled about in the ocean like ball bearings in a turbo, so I'm a bit rattled, that's what's wrong." She shrugged her metallic shoulders stiffly and added, "It's nothing to worry about. The salt water seized my joints a bit."

"Perhaps we can find something here to oil you with. Do you know where we are? Did much of the boat survive?"

"We drifted in on a fragment of the boat. I don't know what happened to it."

He sighed. "It's far from ideal, but we need to find whatever pieces we can, then try to put some sort of boat together."

A leafy creeping vine from the wall broke free and undulated towards them. Instinctively, Orin slapped it away and it retracted. He slumped back on his elbows, feeling suddenly dizzy. "I'm seeing things."

"You're not. It's been doing that since we got here. This whole place is alive with strange moving things."

"Wait, does it have a living, breathing Eard, just like . . . home?" He looked around, amazed.

A girl strode into the room. Orin recognized her emerald eyes as belonging to the girl from the beach. Her clothes were simple but finely made: a beige, short-sleeved, hooded jerkin, arm wraps, and leggings. It wasn't dissimilar to the sort of clothes West Tippers would wear, except hers were soft looking, less rugged and worn than the heavy practical clothes and capes of Ironhold.

"You're awake!" She put a palm to his head.

He flinched away, wary. "Where am I?"

"Heart Tree, in Natura."

He wracked his brain for any memory of the name. Was it an island from Grandma's book? "*Where?*"

"You have a fever, but it's not as high as it was."

"Where are my clothes? Are there any large pieces of my boat left?"

"Your clothes are being washed. You'll get them back."

She spoke the same language as Ironhold, but the sound was different. The *E*s were longer and the *R*s seemed to drop off the end of her words.

He nodded. "Thank you." He noticed she hadn't answered his question about the boat, though, which added to the pit of dread building in his stomach.

"Where are you from?"

He hesitated, not wanting to give too much information away. "An island."

She leant in, her eyes bright with interest. "They

95

say there are no other islands for a great distance. You must have come a very long way. What's your island called?"

"Ironhold."

She repeated the word, exaggerating the form of the word in her mouth. "I've heard rumours of such a place. They call it the mechanical island. What's it like? What did you see on your journey?"

But Orin didn't want to talk about his journey; he wanted to get home. "My boat," he tried again.

She grasped his wrist, felt his pulse, narrowed her eyes, then took his face in her hands and looked from eye to eye, frowning. "Your pulse is faster than it should be and your eyes are bloodshot, but it will pass." Then, glancing down, she added, "Your companion is shy."

"Believe me, she's not usually this quiet." He was still calculating whether or not to trust the girl, but his gut instinct was telling him he was safe at the moment. "Did you find pieces of my boat? I need to get home as soon as I can."

"Can I?" She gestured to his leg.

He nodded. She spoke swiftly and efficiently, though she still didn't seem to be listening to his questions about the boat.

On the beach he hadn't been in much of a state to notice anything, so while she removed the dressing he studied her face. Her eyebrows were set in a serious line, emerald almond-shaped eyes slightly upturned, her jawline angular, and her skin lighter than his.

"I need to get back to the beach and find pieces of my boat," he said again. "Could you take me there?"

"I'm afraid that's not possible," she replied at last.

Orin steeled himself. The last thing he felt like was a fight, but he had seven days to get home, and he had to allow for time to make repairs. He needed to assess the damage straight away. "I'm going back to the beach this morning whether you take me or not," he said with less force than he'd hoped. His leg throbbed.

Putting her hands up defensively, she said, "You can go back to the beach if you really want."

He nodded, satisfied.

She shrugged, matter-of-factly. "But you won't find anything. I went back there yesterday and whatever you washed ashore on had already been reclaimed by the tide."

Orin looked to Cody in despair. "How are we going to get home?"

The girl pulled the last of the dressing off his leg and he winced in pain. She glanced up briefly and muttered an apology.

The wound was an angry red.

"You're not in any state to travel, anyway. This is a bad cut. I think it's infected." She picked up a large, furry brown sphere, drew a knife from her belt and split it open.

"Then can I borrow one of your boats?" It would be quicker and easier than mending his. "I don't have any credits to pay, but I would bring it back." Maybe he could bring his family here, once he'd rescued them.

The girl breathed out a laugh full of disdain. "Good luck with that. There are no boats on Natura."

"No boats?" Orin swung his feet out of bed. What sort of island didn't have boats? "Look, I need to check the beach. You might have missed something, or pieces might have washed in on the next tide." His head swam and the sudden movement made the blood rush from his wound. His bruised ribs burned.

The girl planted herself in front of him. "What's your name?"

"Orin."

"Listen, Orin from the sea, there *is no boat,* so you might as well stay here and recover, at least for now." She shrugged. "I'm Ferelith."

Brow deeply furrowed with a mix of worry and determination, Orin glanced at Cody. He didn't want to send Cody off on her own in this strange place to search, but... He would talk to her as soon as Ferelith had gone.

Meanwhile, Ferelith had produced a small bronze pummel and had begun grinding the white inside layer of the sphere.

"What's that?"

"Coconut. Don't you have them where you come from?"

He shook his head. He'd never seen or heard of such a thing. She began spreading the oily paste on his wound. Wincing, he swallowed and tried to disguise the pain he was in. He looked to the wall. A motion caught his eye, as a creeper moved again.

"You have an Eard?"

Her eyes became suddenly wide and interested. "Do you have one too? It's rumoured there are others."

"Yes, but it doesn't make rooms, like this."

"Really? Then what does it do?"

"Well ... it keeps the island stable." He wasn't sure if that was the right word. Commander Forge had always been secretive about it, saying it was essential to their way of life, and that her connection to it was crucial.

"Have this." Ferelith passed him a green bottle.

"What is it?" he asked suspiciously. An image of the vials of life-light back on Ironhold flashed through his mind.

"Water. I'm not trying to poison you." She tutted.

Orin weighed up the situation. This girl didn't *seem* threatening. He took the water and drank gratefully. There was a jauntiness to the way she spoke. Some of her sentences seemed to rise at the end like questions, even though they weren't.

Ferelith glanced at Orin. "What is your silver creature friend? She's beautiful, like the stars. I've never seen anything like her. I've heard stories. . ."

"Stories?" It sounded odd to hear her talk about something as familiar as a fixie as though it was from a story. "It's a fixie. They're made of azothe. It's a super-flexible metal."

"My name is Cody."

Crouching, Ferelith looked Cody up and down with wonder. "It's lovely and fascinating to meet you, Cody." She looked back to Orin. "You must tell me more about your home, but first, do you think you can stand up? Let me help."

"I can do it myself, I'm all right."

"You're stubborn, not all right."

Cody sniggered and Orin threw her a glare. It was exactly the sort of thing Cody would have said to him.

He managed to stand and take one step, then another before the world tilted, then his legs wobbled and his knees gave way. Ferelith grabbed one arm and a thick vine shot from the ceiling, wrapped around his other arm, and hoisted him back to standing.

He stared at the vine looping his arm. This Eard was so active! So different to the subtle moves of the Eard back home.

"Steady, it's just the blood rushing," said Ferelith.

She observed him with focused eyes, half-grinning. "Your eyes are as large as coconuts."

"I'm fine, feeling better with every moment." All he could think about was the boat. He had to pretend he felt well, even if he didn't.

"Good, because everyone's waiting."

"Waiting? For what?"

She gave another of her matter-of-fact shrugs. "The trial."

CHAPTER 9

"A trial?" Orin screeched before he had time to control his alarm. They had trials on Ironhold. Not often, because everything ran like clockwork, but last year a man from West Tip had stolen a whole crop of beans from one of the cultivation towers, and he'd been locked away in the reparation tower. Grandpa said no one would be seeing him again. "But I'm not a criminal! I just accidentally washed up on your island."

"I'm supposed to take you to my uncle," Ferelith said. "Come on."

They emerged from the entwined root space into a leaf-covered oasis of dappled sunshine and dripping emerald vines. It was as though Orin and

Ferelith were still inside an enormous tree. But that was impossible; trees weren't that big, not in the gardens of Ironhold. "There's so much green," he breathed.

A different girl sat on a rock several metres away, sharpening a knife. Orin didn't notice her at first, as her root-coloured jerkin and trousers blended into the interlaced branches behind her. Dark brown hair was pulled back tightly in a braid which rested on her shoulder, and her suntanned face was dusted with freckles. She watched him with suspicious amber eyes. There was a similarity to Ferelith in that they shared the same serious line to their eyebrows and the square-shaped face, but this girl's eyes were narrower. As they walked towards her, sparks flew from the flint landing close to his feet.

"Who's she?" Orin whispered to Ferelith. She was a little older than Ferelith and had a look of authority in her glare and the severity and strength of her shoulders. Around her waist she wore a belt with several knife pouches of different sizes.

Ferelith laughed and whispered, "She's just my cousin, Nara. Don't mind her, she likes to think she's important, because of her father. She was with me when we found you on the beach."

The effort of walking left Orin shaking. The girl called Nara didn't get up, and he was glad of Ferelith supporting his elbow. He was worried about what he was walking into, what being on trial actually meant. But these people were his only hope of getting home.

Beaming, Ferelith gestured to him as though she'd caught a prize fish. "Nara, I know his name. It's Orin."

By contrast, Nara observed him as though he was rotten kelp that had washed ashore. "The boy spat out by the sea," she said slowly, running her thumb along the flat of the blade she was sharpening.

Orin swallowed. This girl didn't like him at all. Well, good, if she didn't like him, she might help him work out how to get home and then they would never have to see each other again.

Nara sheathed her knife firmly. "Thao's waiting outside."

The hairs on the back of Orin's neck rose. "If it's all the same, I need to get to the beach and see if any of my boat survived. I have to get home."

"Quiet," said Nara.

Orin bristled at her tone, but obeyed.

Ferelith leant in and whispered, "He's from the mechanical island. It's called ... *Ironhold*." She spread her arms as she declared the word, but Nara showed little interest.

Cody peered out from behind Orin's leg.

"I gathered." Nara stared scornfully at Cody and Orin, her gaze moving up and down them like a scythe. "Nothing this freakish would be of Natura. The islands south of here haven't bothered us in ages."

"Look at her outer shell; the material is nothing like we have here. Aren't you even a little interested?"

Nara shook her head and flashed a sour glance at Ferelith, but Orin noticed Ferelith's eyes were lit with curiosity.

"No, and neither should you be."

Ferelith turned to Orin. "I can understand you want to look for your boat, but I promise there was no sign of it on the beach. Besides, you're too ill to go anywhere. When you're better, perhaps we can help—"

Tutting, Nara stood up. "Like I said, Thao is waiting outside."

Ferelith drew herself up. She was smaller than

Nara, but her shoulders were drawn back and her stance firm.

Nara gave an ill-tempered grunt, pushed back the vines and disappeared.

"You'll get used to her," said Ferelith.

"I don't plan on sticking around long enough."

"We need to go and see Thao."

"Is he your commander?"

She looked puzzled.

"Your leader. The one with a special link to the Eard. With the mark?" If they had an Eard, they must have a custodian too.

"Oh, sort of, but not really. There's only one leader of Natura, and that's the Eard."

Frowning, Orin wondered how that could be possible. How could it make even the simplest decisions?

He followed Ferelith through the dripping vines and twisted roots, his heart in his mouth. After a short distance, they reached a firmer section of thick bark wall and passed through a gap, emerging into bright early-morning sunlight. They were now in the open air. Above, enormous branches arced and swayed, silver leaves glistened, and as Orin spun to look back, he saw they *had* been inside of a tree. And this was no ordinary tree: its trunk was as thick as the Engineerium tower. Orin looked up again: it seemed to reach as high too, the huge branches and silvery leaves spread out like an enormous umbrella canopy above. They would surely reach the clouds, Orin thought. A waterfall spouted from one of the mid-branches, sending ice-clear water into a pool; and those glistening leaves! He blinked in bewilderment. As if the silver leaves weren't enough, the bark appeared to pulse in a slow undulation, which he could only compare to his own breath rising and falling in his chest.

"This is Heart Tree," said Ferelith.

"I told you silver is superior," said Cody, smiling at Orin.

"This is quite something. Imagine what Mum, Dad and Grandpa would think of this!" His stomach squeezed at the thought of them and how worried they would be.

They stood on the raised root area at the base of the Heart Tree. Slowly, Orin turned to take in what else was here. They seemed to be in the centre of an enormous valley full of thousands of smaller trees.

Orin's jaw gaped in bewilderment. Back home most of the trees were grown under strict conditions in the botanical garden sector. Here they were wild and free and absolutely everywhere. He wondered where people actually lived; there didn't seem to be space for houses with all the trees. Perhaps there weren't many people? But then he noticed there were lots busying around the valley. He hadn't noticed them at first because they wore muted earthy colours: greens, beiges and browns which blended in with the land. Those closest began to look over at him curiously.

"Where does everyone live?" he asked. "Are the houses outside the valley?"

"I don't know what houses are, but the smaller trees are homes," said Ferelith.

"You live in trees?"

"Of course. Where else would we live?"

"Actually inside the trees?" He couldn't believe it.

"Sounds like your ideal home," said Cody.

"There are pods and spaces within the wide trunks of the valley trees, just like Heart Tree but on a smaller scale. The Eard grows them specially."

There was so much to take in. Around the tree-filled valley, circling the perimeter, were more trees, except larger, of similar height to the centre tree but slightly thinner and with regular green leaves, and some of these great plants seemed to have grown in what appeared to be the shape of human beings, their heads so high up they reached wisps of low-level cloud.

Orin had to check his eyes weren't playing tricks on him. "Do those look like people to you, Cody?"

"They look like giants."

"The Eard grows them too," said Ferelith matter-of-factly.

Orin felt as though he had fallen into a dream, composed of curves, twists and earthy tones rather than the straight lines and metallic hues of Ironhold. Clearly nature ruled in Natura; it was wild and beautiful. Magical, almost.

"It's incredible," he breathed. The Eard here was free and uninhibited. It was everywhere.

Then he noticed more people staring nearby and beginning to gather around Heart Tree, and thoughts of the trial returned and dragged him down like gravity. The dream was about to turn into a nightmare.

"Heart Tree is the centre of the Eard," said

Ferelith. "We think of this tree as the heart, but the Eard's roots and branches extend across the island. Is it different with your Eard?"

He nodded awkwardly, thinking of how contained their Eard was, hidden away underneath the Engineerium, used by Commander Forge and her engineers for its precious life-light. "Does your Eard have life-light?" When she frowned, he added, "The glittery blood."

She laughed. "Oh, you mean its soul?"

He nodded. He guessed that's what it was, though the idea of it made what Commander Forge was doing even more sinister.

"Yes, it especially likes to show its lights at night!"

"But no one here ... you know, takes it out of the Eard?"

Pausing, she glared. "Of course not. That would be unthinkable."

Ferelith led Orin and Cody around the base of the Heart Tree until they reached a bearded man about Orin's father's age, who was sitting on a large raised root looking contemplative. He wore a sand-coloured, short-sleeved jerkin and trousers, mittens that stretched from his knuckles to his elbows, and

III

had strong muscles that made Orin aware of his own slim, immature frame. When the man heard them approaching, he looked up. He had an air of stillness and a strength that reminded Orin of a sturdy tree he had seen in the botanical gardens back on Ironhold: an oak.

"Uncle." Ferelith nodded respectfully. "Orin, this is Thao, head of the people of Natura. Uncle, this is Orin. He's from the mechanical island of Ironhold." She said the name as though it was a precious jewel.

"Orin Crowfall," Orin added, thinking that his full name sounded more official somehow, and less like a washed-up, ragtag boy from the West Tip. He wanted to make a good impression, because if anyone could help him here, it would hopefully be this man. Thao had the same bright green eyes as Ferelith, and his brow was engraved with wisdom. His hair, long and brown, was half-tied back. "Sir..." He paused and corrected himself. "Sorry, Commander? Er ... how should I address you?"

"Thao. We only have one name on Natura. I am head of the people, but I do not command." His voice was deep, quiet, yet imposing. "So, you're from the mechanical island, Orin? The place that controls nature instead of appreciating and respecting its power."

"Yes, sir, I mean, Thao." Orin nodded, biting his tongue while keeping his head respectfully dipped.

An amused slant edged Thao's lips for a fleeting moment. "Why have you come here?"

Sweat dampened Orin's palms. "I didn't exactly come on purpose. I was in a boat, there was a storm and. . ." He paused, thinking it best he didn't mention the mechanical sea monster, since it had been created to keep outsiders like them away from Ironhold. "I crashed into this water forest place, and nearly drowned, and then I woke up on your beach. This is my friend, she's called Cody, she pulled me to shore."

Bending down, Thao looked curiously at Cody, who blinked and took a step back.

"Don't worry, I won't hurt you, little one. You must be strong to have pulled him up the beach."

Cody nodded. "Fixies are twice as strong. We're built to do lots of construction and fixing on Ironhold."

Thao studied Orin again.

"Sir, if you'll just help me, I'll be gone tomorrow, or as soon as I'm able. Really, there's no need for this trial. I'm feeling better with every moment. I'll just. . ."

A woman appeared from one of the natural doorways in the trunk of Heart Tree close by, followed by Nara. She had the same suspicious eyes and dark brown hair pulled tightly off her face in a braid.

"Saviri," Thao acknowledged.

"My aunt," Ferelith mouthed to Orin.

Saviri's eyes darted briefly to Orin, then back to Thao, her lips tight. *Great*, Orin thought; two people who already didn't like him, and there was an increasingly large group of people gathering around Heart Tree looking at him as though he was a new species. This didn't exactly bode well.

"There will be a trial. Let's gather all the people," Thao said, walking to the edge to look over the clearing. He took what looked to be a wooden horn from his belt and put it to his lips, and a low call echoed through the valley.

"What exactly does the trial involve?" Orin asked Ferelith.

After a concentrated frown, Ferelith took a breath. "The Eard decides if you can stay or not."

Cody looked up at Orin. "That doesn't sound too arduous."

Ferelith's lips twisted awkwardly for a moment, as though she was deciding whether to hold back from saying something. "The thing is, I think … when people have come before, they have had a boat for when they get thrown back into the sea."

"Thrown back into the sea?" The words lurched from his mouth.

"You'd have to leave immediately."

Orin's stomach felt suddenly heavier. What was this place? Were they so completely heartless that they could abandon a boy to the sea without a boat?

Cody looked up with her big eyes. "Looks like you're going to have to persuade them to let us stay for a bit. Best turn on that human charm of yours."

Orin rolled his eyes. "Thanks for that wisdom, pal." But he could tell that beneath her sarcasm she was worried.

The people of Natura gathered in the space before Heart Tree. If this was the entire population of the island, it was much smaller than Ironhold, perhaps as little as a tenth, Orin thought. Surely one small boy could stay for a few days to find and fix a boat.

Ushering Orin to the centre, Thao addressed the

crowd. "We will commence the cleansing shortly, but as you are aware, we have a stranger in our midst. This boy is Orin, from the mechanical island, washed up on Natura by chance."

There was a mistrustful hiss from the crowd when Thao said the words "mechanical island". Orin shrank back into his shoulders. They seemed to hate outsiders as much as Ironholders did.

"As the rules dictate, a trial is the appropriate action for outsiders, so that his fate can be decided by the Eard." The crowd nodded their agreement.

Orin couldn't believe his fate was going to be decided by the Eard. He wondered again how the Eard could make a decision one way or the other. It was a living organism, sure, but it couldn't communicate to such a sophisticated level. Could it?

"The people from that island are dangerous," a woman in the crowd called. "They don't respect nature, they cover it with grey! Imagine how they would treat an Eard if they had one!"

There were mutters of agreement. Orin thought it probably wasn't the best time to tell the crowd they actually did have an Eard, too.

"Who knows what bad fortune he will bring?"

said a young man.

Orin felt the sudden urge to defend himself and Ironhold. These people knew nothing about his home – how wonderful it was, in its own ways. How dare they? He stepped forward. "It's not true! Our cultivation towers and gardens are incredible. We do work with nature, controlling it to make it better because our population is large. Our engineers are the best you could imagine. We can turn seawater to freshwater with our machines, and power our city with generators."

Thao raised a hand at Orin. "I'm sorry, but you're not allowed to speak unless invited to."

"Why not? I'm the one on trial!"

"Get on with it and throw him back where he came from," someone shouted.

"Into the sea!"

Orin stepped forward again. "Look, all I want to do is go home. There's really no need for this trial. If you could lend me a boat, maybe a weapon."

A collective gasp discharged from the crowd.

"He wants a weapon!"

"The boy wishes us harm!"

"He's just a child. We can't just throw him back

into the sea!" a young woman called. Orin was relieved to see a small group nod along in agreement.

"What harm could he do?" added another.

"Maybe we should give him time to make a raft?"

"The mechanical people only take," Saviri said loudly.

Thao put a hand on hers. "The Eard will decide his fate. Ferelith? It is time."

"Fate?" Orin whispered to Ferelith. "What happens now?"

"If the Eard lets you walk the bridge, you can stay." She pointed diagonally upwards.

Orin looked to where she pointed. "What do you mean?" he whispered, alarmed. "There isn't a bridge."

CHAPTER 10

Steadying his nerves, Orin followed Ferelith as she turned and walked back towards Heart Tree. His pulse pounded and beads of sweat prickled his skin as he climbed up the inside of the tree. Not only did Heart Tree have spaces at ground level within the trunk, but it also had spaces to climb within: stairways of twisted wood spiralling up and up. Cody hadn't been permitted to join them, as Thao said she fell outside of the rules of the trial. Orin still didn't like to think of her alone in this strange, hostile place, but at least she would be safe from being cast out to sea.

Eventually, he and Ferelith emerged on a high branch. From this height he could see the entirety of the valley and the island edges, equally lush with trees and plants, with open meadow areas and forests, rising areas at the edge along with a few beaches and glistening blue sea beyond. Orin wasn't afraid of heights, though looking down at the many people far below, now just a speckled mass of tiny dots staring silently upwards, made his head spin.

"What now?" he said, trying to keep the alarm out of his voice.

"You walk out to the end of the branch and step off."

"You've got to be kidding!" This was ridiculous. Why would he do that? He didn't have to follow their stupid rules.

"If the Eard wants you to stay, it won't let you fall."

This was all some hideous nightmare. Right now he'd rather take his chances with the mechanical sea monster. "If your Eard doesn't catch me, I'll break my legs, probably die, and then it won't matter if I'm thrown into the sea!" He turned around. "I think I'll skip this part and just go straight to the beach."

Grasping his shoulders, Ferelith spun him round again. "Even if the Eard lets you fall, it will probably cushion your landing a little."

"How many outsiders have ever passed this trial?"

She hesitated. "Well... Thao says that people would come and go more freely when his parents were young, one a week, but there have been none for fifty years now."

Panic widened Orin's eyes and his mouth gaped. The odds were definitely not in his favour.

"Come on." She gave him a gentle push. "We need to get this done before the cleansing bells. I shouldn't really be up here with you."

Shakily, he took a step forward. Death by falling, or death by drowning. Perhaps drowning would be better. At least it might not be so painful. Moving to turn back, he almost lost his footing and flailed his arms wildly.

"Concentrate!" Ferelith hissed.

He decided to sit and edge his way towards the end of the branch.

"Now stand and step," Ferelith instructed. "I've got to go back down, good luck!" Her voice faded away.

The branch tapered as he moved forwards, and it was barely the width of his feet now. Carefully, giving every inch of concentration to his balance, he pushed himself up.

He heard the crowd below start to murmur: "*Step! Step! Step!*"

He shut his eyes. What else could he do except throw wild hope into the ether? He lifted his left foot, then extended it. *Please save me.*

Then he stepped.

His foot fell freely. Stomach met throat and the hideous lurch of free fall swallowed him. *Let it not be painful.* The crowd gasped. His heart somersaulted as his body tilted forward with the fall.

Then, before he'd barely started tumbling, his foot hit something solid. He launched his hands out and found what felt like branches. From somewhere below, he heard Ferelith let out a squeal of delight. Orin opened his eyes to see the branch had magically extended a little way to form a wider platform, with branches twisting upwards to form spindles and railings, just like a natural bridge. Below, gasps of wonder, grunts of disbelief, and huffs of relief rose in a dissonant exhalation of noise.

"Take more steps!" called Ferelith. He lifted his other foot and took another step, this time watching. There was a gentle creak as the branch grew beneath him and let him walk. It extended again as he took step after step.

Somewhere in the crowd, Thao called, "The Eard says he stays!"

The bridge began to turn and spiral downwards, forming before his eyes until he wound his way back down to the ground again. A rush of elation filled him. He couldn't believe what had just happened. He'd been saved!

By the time he stepped off, Cody was there to greet him, clapping with ferocious glee. The feeling of relief was like jumping in a cool pool on the hottest day of his life. But what now? Did this mean they would help him to get home?

Ferelith grinned at him widely. "The Eard must like you!"

For a moment, Orin felt like some sort of celebrity as the crowd chattered excitedly and pointed at him. This must be how Commander Forge felt when she addressed Ironhold, he thought, and then his stomach turned at the thought of the commander and what she was doing to their own Eard. And what would happen to Ironhold and everyone in it if he didn't get back in time to stop her.

The crowd began to disperse, Nara and her mother shooting him barbed glances as they left. He noticed a few other sneering looks too. It seemed that even though the Eard had allowed him to stay, some people's opinion of Ironhold, and what he stood for, remained.

Ringing filled the air, coming from above, and Orin looked up to see the silver leaves quivering to cause the sound.

Ferelith hurried away. "It's time for the morning cleansing. I haven't got my equipment!"

"But you need to take me to the beach to look for my boat. Can I get help now the Eard has accepted me?"

Turning towards him, she smiled. "Sit and rest here by the Heart Tree waterfall for a moment. I need to get my stuff, then we can talk while we're cleansing."

Now the adrenaline was wearing off, Orin realized how much his leg hurt and was grateful to sit down. The waterfall flowed from the trunk about a third of the way up Heart Tree. The water gathered in a small pool at its base, then ran in a small river which meandered through the valley. Still sweating from the trial, he was grateful to feel the delicate cold spray of water on his skin.

Cody sat beside him. "You didn't fall! I was certain you'd be flatter than a solar disc by now."

"So was I. But you're not getting rid of me that easily."

"Chance would be a fine thing." Cody nudged him playfully.

Orin thought about the beaches he'd seen from the tree. "Maybe we should just go and see if we can find the beach ourselves." Although he couldn't be certain which beach to check first.

"Orin, you're still weak. I know we need to get home, but it's going to be easier if we can get this girl to help us. She seems to want to."

"I suppose you're right." Although Ferelith certainly didn't seem to realize the importance of getting back to the beach as soon as possible.

A few millidays later, Ferelith returned. She carefully laid out a bright white cloth, and upon it placed a large silver bowl, a shiny ladle and some more neatly folded cloths. She went to the waterfall and filled the bowl.

Frowning, Orin saw that everyone in the valley

was doing the same thing beside the trees. Even Thao. Sitting next to her bowl, Ferelith added a few drops of oil from a silver vial, mixed it with her hand and muttered some words under her breath. Then she took a ladle and scooped the water, stood and spooned it on to a low branch.

"What are you doing?" asked Orin as she dipped the cloth in the water again and began washing an area of the trunk.

"We have a daily cleansing to keep the Eard well. It looks after us, so we look after it. Don't you do that on your island?"

He shook his head. Only Commander Forge interacted with their Eard. How they treated their Eard was so different.

"Would you like to help? The Eard did allow you to stay; you should probably thank it."

He nodded. It seemed a strange way to thank it, but then what did he know?

"How does the Eard look after you?"

"It provides food, water, makes our homes. Everything."

So much work went into the careful growing and distribution of crops in Ironhold, Orin couldn't imagine endless supplies just by thanking the Eard. It struck him that while that was kind of the Eard, there wasn't much satisfaction in being handed everything instantly and not nurturing it yourself. Maybe that was why the people of Natura performed these rituals.

"Here, ladle the leaves there. It'll like that."

With a frown, he dipped a ladle into the water, then trickled it on to the leaves nearby. They fluttered happily. "How about the trees shaped like people? Are they part of the Eard, or did you make them?" Orin thought they were incredible, like wild and organic giant humans. "They don't come to life and walk or anything weird, do they?"

Cody giggled.

"What? It's a valid question," Orin said defensively, although he felt a bit daft having suggested it.

"No, they're just the images of important people from our past. Those who work closest with the Eard. The Eard has the ability to sculpt and shape itself. One day a tree shaped as Uncle Thao will stand there."

How could this island be so very different to

Ironhold? Here the Eard seemed to have a will, and connected with all the people, not just one, and even had authority over them. Back home the Eard was hidden from all but the Core.

"So what does Crowfall mean? Your other name?"

"It's my surname. We have two names on Ironhold."

"Why?"

"To show our heritage, I guess."

"Why?"

He shrugged. "To show where we come from."

"But it can't tell you where you're going."

"She's not wrong there," said Cody. "I don't have a second name, so does that disadvantage me somehow, too?"

Orin frowned, unsure of what to make of the conversation.

"Perhaps you could tell me about this Crowfall name and where you come from?"

Then the silver leaves chimed and Ferelith jumped up. "There, we're finished."

"Great, then we can go and check the beach."

She paused. "I told you, I went to look yesterday and there wasn't anything."

"There's a chance something might have washed ashore today."

She sighed. "All right. It's harvesting after cleansing anyway. Come with me and we can go check the beach while we're out."

Orin gave a nod of acknowledgement, but he couldn't help feeling a sense of unease at her reluctance. He shook it off. It didn't matter. He needed help, and she was his only option.

CHAPTER II

Orin's legs and ribs still ached and his head felt hot, but he followed Ferelith as best he could through Heart Tree's various tunnels and rooms. "What's harvesting?" he asked her. He'd heard the term from books about early farming, when growing mainly took place outside in Ironhold, before the population grew too big and they needed the space for housing. Certain crops could only be gathered once a year, which they called the annual harvest. But since the invention of the cultivation towers, everything was grown all year round.

"It's what we call our daily picking routine."

After packing up her cleansing equipment, Ferelith took a basket and they left Heart Tree.

They passed trees with homes tucked inside, and he noticed other people carrying baskets too, presumably also to gather food. Orin thought it was nice to see people so relaxed, and spending time together. In Ironhold, you got food from distributors by paying credits that you earned from your job. Everyone had a role to keep the system working.

"The best berries are deep in the forest on the west of the island – well, this year, anyway. It's not too far, and there are some things I'd like to show you there. The beach is close by."

"So you don't grow anything yourselves? The Eard does it *all* for you?"

Nonplussed, Ferelith nodded. "Of course. The Eard grows all we need. We'd never do as good a job of it, and it would be disrespectful. We don't want it to think we're ungrateful."

Orin and Cody exchanged a glance. It didn't seem quite right to Orin to rely so heavily on the Eard for everything. He was surprised they hadn't found a way to get the Eard to pick it all for them, too.

They wove onwards through the village. Each family appeared to have its own small tree, and natural leafy routes wove around them. The river running from the waterfall of Heart Tree flowed to the east and children played in it and adults gathered water in ceramic jugs. The people he passed were still looking curiously at him and Cody, but he tried to ignore that and focus on taking in the details of this incredible island and the way its people lived. He noticed some people exchanging supplies: a knitted blanket for a pair of trousers, a carved wooden toy for a jug. There certainly didn't seem to be a system of credits.

They reached the great statue trees and entered the thick green of the forest. The going was slow, as Orin had to keep pausing to catch his breath and sitting down to rest on rocks to ease the pain in his leg. But he was determined to get to the beach.

They zigzagged through the winding stems, green-furred trunks, rocks crusted with lichen, and branches dripping with white moss. They stopped at a brook to drink. The trees echoed with croaks, tribbles and warbles. There was a sweetness to the earthy scent of the deep forest. Orin wondered if any crows lived here, or if the islanders had chased them away, too.

"How much further to the beach?"

"Not far. But we'll stop for the berries first. There are some here already, like these," Ferelith announced, pointing at a clump of glossy black fruits. Then she looked at him and paused. "Actually, maybe we should head back. You're not looking great. Maybe this was too much, too soon." She frowned.

"You *are* looking rather peaky," Cody said.

Orin's leg throbbed and he saw his wound was bleeding through the bandage. But he didn't want to admit how bad he felt because all he could think was that he only had seven days to save his family. "I'm fine, I'll just rest a moment," he said, as a fresh wave of pain surged.

Cody looked doubtfully at him, then scanned the forest. "There are some plump ones up there. I'll climb to the high branches; we'll be quicker that way."

"Be careful. Remember, you don't have wings if you fall."

"That's interesting, coming from you." Cody shook her head, then scurried up into the branches.

While Ferelith gathered fruit close by, it seemed to Orin to be a good time to find out more about her, including something he'd been wondering since this morning. "You haven't told me yet."

"Told you what?"

"Why you saved me when pretty much everyone else here would have thrown me straight back in the sea."

When she looked at him, her emerald eyes shone with an inner glow. "I guess I was intrigued when you landed on the beach." She turned and carried on picking berries. Orin wondered whether she was going to continue. After a moment she looked back to him. "I'm not sure why I'm telling you this, but have you ever felt as though you're in a box, and . . . it's a nice enough box, but it . . . doesn't feel like yours? Maybe you want to be in a different box . . . or lots of different ones. But everyone keeps telling you, *no*, this is your box. Like . . . destiny has you all wrong. So you start to accept it and then something happens, like a stranger from another island lands on a beach and you just happen to be near, and it's as though, perhaps, destiny hasn't forgotten you." Shaking her head and looking at the forest floor, she added, "Forget it, I sound stupid."

Orin understood *exactly* what she meant; it was almost as though she'd stepped into his head. So even though he'd only spoken about it with Cody before, he found himself saying, "It's like the crows."

Ferelith frowned. "Crows?"

Poking her head through the branches above, Cody said, "He's obsessed with them."

"Do you have them here?"

Ferelith nodded.

His heart quickened. "Destiny is like the crows, I mean. Sometimes, at home, I go to the cliffs to imagine how the crows must have looked, flying through the sky. They haven't been seen in Ironhold for hundreds of years, because of something my family did, and it was supposed to be a good thing, but. . ." He paused, not ready to reveal that part of his heritage. "But I need to keep hoping they *will* come, because it means something. Sort of. . . That my story doesn't have to be *that* – there's a whole world out there to discover, and it can be anything I want."

"Yes!"

"So what box don't you want to be in?" he asked. "Things seem pretty good here, kind of free."

The stiffening of her shoulders caught his attention. "Aren't they?"

"Not always, but what about for you?"

"West Tippers don't get much freedom at all."

"What are West Tippers?"

"It's the area I'm from in Ironhold, the poorest bit."

"Poor? What's that?"

It struck Orin that, living in Natura, people would have no concept of needing to use credits for everything. Everyone had what they needed and did jobs together. Not like in Ironhold, where people just had one job and did the same thing day after day after day. "It's when some people have less."

"Why?"

It was a good question and one he couldn't answer, so he shrugged and started to help pick berries. "In Ironhold we have tools to help with picking different fruit. It would be much quicker."

"I could make you one," called Cody, climbing down.

"There don't seem to be as many to pick lately. It's strange." She frowned deeply. "Perhaps the Eard needs more from us."

A shaft of sunlight flashed on the hinges where Cody's wings used to be attached, and Orin felt a rush of sadness.

"It's a beautiful view up there," Cody said. "It's a shame you can't climb at the moment. Now, if you were made of azothe, you'd be much tough—" She stopped as a tiny flower-like flying creature flew towards Orin. He went to shoo it away, suddenly worried it might be harmful – after all, he still didn't know much about this island – but Ferelith put a hand out to stop him.

"Relflings are kind."

The electric-blue creature landed before him. It was the most peculiar thing because Orin was sure he could hear whispered words coming from the relfling, although he couldn't understand them.

"They are messengers of the Eard," said Ferelith. "We don't understand their language, but they pass messages from the Eard to creatures."

"Like what?" he asked, fascinated. There were so many amazing things to discover about Natura.

"Things about the island, about each other. All creatures, insects, and even micro-organisms play a role in the ecosystem here. They co-exist and balance each other, so isn't it natural that they communicate? Isn't your island like that?"

"Not exactly," said Cody. "Humans like order on

Ironhold, perhaps even more than the robots who are programmed to be that way. Some of the robots," she corrected.

Balance was a lovely thought to Orin. It was how things should be, harmonious rather than always thinking about meeting quotas and allowances. Orin wished he could understand the language of Ironhold's Eard. Then he might be able to save it. "Can you take a picture of the relfling and save it to your files, please, Cody? I'd like to draw one in Grandma's book when we get home."

After asking the relfling if it minded, Cody's eyes flashed and she committed a picture to her memory bank.

"We really should get to the beach," Orin said.

"I wanted to show you something," Ferelith declared suddenly. Orin couldn't help feeling she kept distracting him. Why didn't she want to go to the beach?

"Well, this will help. Do you remember how you got to Heart Tree?"

He shook his head.

Cupping her mouth, Ferelith let out a deep moaning sound, like the one Orin remembered from the beach, and he resisted the urge to giggle.

"What did you just do?"

She shrugged. "I called a bog myrtle. There's one just over there."

Close by, a group of large, mossy rocks lifted slowly. Orin jolted in surprise, then watched as it, whatever *it* was, took form: a broad, boulder-like back; thick arms and gnarled fingers; head set into the hunch of its shoulders; grey, moss-clagged skin. It clung on to a thin tree trunk and stared at him with doleful, hesitant eyes.

"Well, that's not something you see every day," Cody said, and nudged Orin.

"What is it?" Orin breathed, taking a step back. The creature was around one-and-a-half times the height of him. There were few creatures on Ironhold – bees kept for honey and pollination, dogs and cats owned by engineers, the rats of West Tip – but little else, and certainly nothing like this!

"A bog myrtle – they're peaceful and perfectly harmless. They like the edges of the island, where it's quietest. They're pretty fast when they get going."

He gave her a disbelieving glance; it looked more lumbering than speedy to him.

"I've picked as many berries as I can find, and you wanted to look for wood on the beach; let's go for a ride."

"A ride? On that?"

"You've already done it once. You might have been unconscious, but you still did it." She took a step forward. "Come on, there's nothing to be afraid of."

"I'm not afraid," Orin squeaked, thinking this thing could most certainly crush a person.

"Err, I was talking to the bog myrtle."

Cody's shoulders shook with a silent giggle.

Tentatively, the bog myrtle left the tree and went down on all four rocky limbs. Ferelith stroked it enthusiastically on the head and beneath the chin. "There, who's a lovely little boggy? Shall we go for a ride? Shall we?"

She climbed on to its back.

Orin hoisted Cody up, then clambered on himself. The moss on the creature's back was strangely warm, and suddenly he remembered the feeling from the beach.

"Hold on!" Ferelith called. Soon they were hurtling over rocks and between trees, the bog myrtle's legs pounding the ground softly beneath them, leaves rushing past. Shortly they left the leafy forest and rode into bright sunlight. They were close to a clifftop overlooking a beach.

"That's where you washed ashore."

Orin stared out at the enormity of the sea. They'd somehow crossed *that* and survived?

Ironhold was out there. His family was out there. *I'm here,* he said silently into the wind, hoping with every atom that somehow it would magically carry the message back to them.

He scanned the beach, but there was no sign of any boat fragments. "Let's look more closely." He hoped there might be pieces of the wreckage hidden by rocks, or somewhere out of sight.

The bog myrtle took them down to the beach and they began scouring, but Orin was disappointed to recover only a few small pieces, no longer than the length of his arm – nothing big enough to build a boat. Ferelith found a loose vine so he could tie them together in a bundle. Disappointment at the lack of wreckage felt as though a black hole of nothing had opened underneath him. "What do we do?" he asked Cody weakly.

She flipped open her fingers and spun a screwdriver tool. "We get making."

Even if there wasn't any wreckage, there were at least lots of trees around for wood to make a new boat. But it would take them several days with just the two of them. It was day three now, and that left three more to make the boat, three to get back, then one day to find Mum and Dad and Grandpa and escape again. They walked further along the beach, Orin still hopeful that some larger pieces of the boat would appear but resigned to the fact they would need to work quickly.

In the distance, figures hunched on the shoreline looking downwards.

"Are they collecting seaweed?" asked Orin.

"Whatever for?" Ferelith looked bemused.

"Eating, of course." He paused before he remembered the Eard provided all the food on Natura. On Ironhold any food the Eard provided was limited and just for the Core. He wondered if the way it was restrained meant it couldn't produce much.

Ferelith looked at him strangely. "They're scouring for sacred stones."

He frowned. "Sacred stones?"

She put a hand in her jerkin pocket and pulled out a palm-sized, perfectly spherical black stone. "I found this the day I found you. We give them at the offering ceremony."

"Oh. What do they do?"

Ferelith shrugged and passed it to Orin. "The Eard likes them."

The leaves at the beach edge seemed to whisper their approval.

"How do you know it likes them?"

"You'll see later. If it's happy, we know, and if it's not . . . well, we know that too."

That sounded ominous. Orin studied the stone. "It's . . . very round," he said. It didn't make a lot of sense to him, but there was something of a nurturing, two-way, peaceful relationship between the people of Natura and the Eard which he felt quite envious of.

"These outer trees aren't the Eard, are they?"

"No, why?"

"I need to start making a boat this afternoon and I don't want to accidentally take from the Eard."

"Ah, about that." She stopped dead. "Perhaps you

should follow me."

Orin exchanged a glance with Cody, then they both shrugged and followed Ferelith back into the trees.

"So on Ironhold the Eard isn't actually your leader?"

He shook his head. "No. It's Commander Forge. She's the custodian with the mark, the one with the special connection to the Eard, like Thao."

"Why do you keep talking about a *mark*?"

"You know, the pattern on the hand that shows the leader. I'm not sure what you call it here."

"I don't know what you mean. Uncle Thao doesn't have a mark."

Again it felt like a great void opened at Orin's feet. Thao had been wearing long mittens, so Orin couldn't have seen if he had no mark. In his memory Orin saw the medi-robot doing something to Commander Forge's hand. If Thao was the one with the special connection to the Eard, why didn't he have a mark? Was it possible that Commander Forge had misled them about hers? He glanced at Cody and knew she was wondering the same.

They pushed on through into a clearing.

And stopped dead.

In front of them was a great natural prison: a dome, the size of a large room, grown from the ground of fierce-looking briars with enormous, needle-sharp thorns. In the middle sat a young, sad-looking woman, her hair tangled and loose, her arms scratched, the sleeves and legs of her trousers frayed and torn. She glanced at them, then carried on laying a pile of stones in a pattern where she sat.

There was an awkward twist to Ferelith's mouth as she spoke. "You may find getting wood a little tricky. Because on Natura, stealing is strictly frowned upon by the Eard."

Orin felt an uneasy jolt in his stomach. Like on Ironhold, it looked as though things were never as perfect as they seemed.

CHAPTER 12

After Orin repeatedly insisted on searching another beach, Ferelith gave in and took them to one further west on the island. But after a fruitless search, Orin and Cody returned to Heart Tree dispirited. Orin was weak after the exertion, and the ache in his leg had intensified. He knew that even if he found more pieces of the boat, he wouldn't have the energy to put anything together, and he felt uneasy after seeing the dome prison. If this was what happened when you upset the Eard, he didn't want to cross it. And yet, how else would he get home? In the end, Cody insisted they rest and make an early start the next day.

Orin ate some food, a broth of vegetables and

grains that Ferelith had made, and then she left him to go to what she called the offering ceremony. The number of different ceremonies seemed so odd to him. They were at all times of the day. How did people have time to get anything else done?

Although with the Eard providing everything, he didn't suppose they *needed* to do anything except take what it provided and give thanks.

He changed his dressing, applying some of the coconut paste Ferelith had left him, then, exhausted from the day so far, fell into a deep sleep.

When he woke, the throbbing in his leg had eased and his wound felt cooler. He realized with a jolt that he'd slept through the evening and into the night, not stirring until the half-light of dawn crept through the small gaps in the vines. Six more days left to get back.

Cody was still resting her pod power source. Early on when Orin had first connected the pod within Cody, they had found she became lethargic and weak if she was active for too long, but if she rested it nightly the pod would self-recharge. He gave her a tap and told her he was going to get breakfast and then head back to the beach. Outside his sleeping area were several root-formed tunnels and vine-covered walkways, and he knew how to get back outside Heart Tree, but he wasn't sure exactly where to find Ferelith. As he stood pondering which way to try, he noticed movement at his feet. A shoot grew quickly to the height of his ankle and sprouted a blue flower. Then another grew a few paces in front. A vine from above twisted behind him, stiffened, then nudged him in the back so he moved forward.

"Are you showing me the way?" he said curiously. There was something kind about the gesture, and it seemed at odds with the cruel prison dome he'd seen yesterday. He followed a chain of flowers through one of the entwined-branch tunnels and out into a vine-looped glade where he found a small stream, a twisted-root sleeping pod like his own, and a cooking area with a few pots and gentle fire. He saw Ferelith sitting side-on to him. At first, she didn't notice him. There was something contemplative about her expression, as if she was questioning herself, and he could see disappointment in her shoulder line. But before he could think any more about it, she looked over and her frame changed instantly, brightening. "Awake at last! I was worried yesterday had been too much for you." She tore off a chunk of the bread from a tray beside her and threw it to him, along with a piece of crunchy fruit that the Eard grew obligingly.

"Thanks!" The bread was still warm, with delicious nuts and fruit inside. He had never known food so readily available. Everything in Ironhold was so stringently controlled with credits and growth allocations that you mostly knew what to expect. Here, there was none of the stress of quotas and foraging.

"How are you feeling?"

"The paste you gave me is brilliant. My leg and side feel much better. I want to go and check the beaches again, and also ask permission to fell a tree to start on my boat this morning."

Ferelith paused. "Okaaaay. But there's cleansing, and then it's harvesting, honouring the lake, and the offering ceremony."

Raising his eyebrows, Orin said, "Didn't you just do all that yesterday? I could do with some help searching the island. Please?"

"These are daily rituals here, not something you can just decide not to do." She laughed as though it was madness not to know this. "And now the Eard is letting you stay, you really should be performing all of them as well."

"I won't be here long enough for all that."

She shrugged. "Also, if you want a tree, you'll have to ask Thao."

"I thought you said it was up to the Eard?"

"It is, but Thao has to ask."

"All right... Where do I find him?"

"He's already left to cleanse in the north this morning."

After an exasperated grunt, Orin said, "Then after cleansing, you could take me to search the beaches again?" He was hopeful that the new tide may have brought in the wreckage.

"You should go and look yourself."

"Can't you come?" It would be faster and easier with her as a guide.

"I need to go to the eastern part of the island to harvest, and I doubt you'll find anything there."

"But we didn't go there yesterday. Let's search there. I'll come with you."

Muscles tightened in Ferelith's forehead and jaw. He knew she had tasks to do, and after he'd seen how the Eard punished people here, he didn't want to get her into trouble, but he still needed her help. Plus, he realized, he'd actually enjoyed hanging out with her yesterday. He'd felt like they'd understood one another.

"Please, Ferelith, you're the only person I know here." Six days was all he had left, and if he needed to speak to Thao about getting a tree, he couldn't waste a morning not looking for his boat.

She sighed. "Fine, come if you want."

After the cleansing ceremony, Ferelith, Orin and Cody gathered two large baskets and walked through the eastern end of the village trees. Orin had managed to avoid most of the people after the trial yesterday, but the glances coming his way this morning made it clear that many were still wary of him.

They passed an older teenage boy, who was sweeping the ground outside a house tree. Something in his awkward movement caught Orin's attention, and he noticed that the boy's foot was caught in something. Orin paused and saw that there were roots wrapped tightly around his ankle, tethering him to the ground. The roots would let him go so far, then tug him back.

"That boy's stuck," Orin said to Ferelith.

"It's the bind. A punishment."

"Another one?"

"He probably missed a cleansing ceremony." Ferelith shrugged.

As they moved on and walked to the edge of the main village, Orin couldn't help thinking there was a strange combination of extremes in the Eard of Natura. An all-giving, helpful being, yet one that punished and controlled, often cruelly.

A man picking apples called to them. "Look at this fruit." He was pointing to a branch drooping close by. "It's rotten!"

Ferelith stopped to look.

"Bad luck," he said. "That's what comes of letting outsiders in." He threw Orin an accusatory glare.

"It's nothing to do with me," said Orin, affronted. How could they possibly believe the rotten fruit was his fault? The tree was heavy with apples, and it was clear to him they just weren't picking it quickly enough.

"I have a fair few mouldy fruits here too," said a woman at the next tree.

"Perhaps if you had something to help you pick faster?" suggested Cody, placing a calming hand on Orin's arm.

Orin nodded at her. Now wasn't the time to overreact. In fact, he thought she'd had a good idea. When a large crop needed to be harvested, the cultivators always used an extra robotic arm, to make the most of the harvest while it was good, and so as not to lose any of the produce.

Hurrying over to the apple tree, Cody scurried up, and her arms went into a blur of action as she whizzed through the trees picking and launching the apples into the basket at the man's feet with absolute precision. The man looked befuddled, his eyes darting, unsure, from side to side, then the Eard extended a branch, looped it around the basket handle and lifted it into the man's arms.

"Why, thank you!" the man called to Cody. "I can see there's no bad luck coming from you."

"Come on, we should be on our way," said Ferelith. "I'll have to tell my uncle about the fruit. The Eard must be unhappy."

They crossed into the forest to the east of the village. Here it was less mossy and there were many saplings and giant ferns. As Orin passed one tree, a branch seemed to reach out and tickle him playfully. Caught unawares, he jumped, then laughed. This Eard was so active and surprising. Was there something hiding behind its harshness? Hurt? The people in Ironhold took care of the land, but they had no contact with the Eard itself. In spite of the cruelty he'd seen, here there was a closer relationship between the Eard and its people. It looked after them – and there was something nice about that. He wondered how things might be on Ironhold if they took down the conservatory that contained the Eard and gave it the chance to be free.

"Tell me about your family," said Ferelith.

"There's Mum and Dad; they're called Estri and Caelan. They work cleaning, the fixie factory mostly. Then there's Grandpa; he's called Sol."

"And your grandma?"

"I never knew her, but she was called Merina, and Grandpa said she had a thousand stories in her soul."

"Really? I like the sound of that."

"And you know Cody. She's my best friend. No one back home knows she can speak like she does, though." It was strange, but now he'd told her about the crows, other things came easily when he spoke to Ferelith.

"Why?"

"Fixies are meant to be just robots. Robots aren't meant to have opinions."

"What exactly are robots *meant* to do, then?"

"They're created purely for tasks." He paused and felt his cheeks redden. It had occurred to him that perhaps the people of Natura were a bit robotic in their offerings.

"What about your family?" Orin noticed a sapling close by that had been snapped. He bent to examine it.

"You've met them – Thao, Saviri and Nara." Ferelith crouched beside him, then took the band out of her hair and retied it. "What are you doing?"

"I'm assuming that this one isn't part of the Eard, or it would have mended itself."

"He simply can't pass by a broken plant without saving it," Cody said, shrugging. "You should see his room back on Ironhold. It's full of them."

Orin found a sturdy twig and staked it into the ground beside the sapling. Cody passed some string from her finger supply and he bound it together, leaving a little give so that it could both heal and grow.

"My parents died when I was three."

He looked up at Ferelith, but she was now gazing into the distance. "I'm sorry."

"I don't remember much of them at all."

"What happened?" Orin asked tentatively. He finished tying off the string, and Cody used one of her finger tools to snip the string end neatly.

Ferelith looked back down at him. "They broke the rules." Seeing the shock on his face, she added, "Oh, they weren't killed or anything. The Eard punishes but doesn't kill. They wanted to explore and broke the rules. Their boat upturned and they died at sea."

"That's awful." It was similar to what happened to his grandmother, though the Sentinel was to blame, really. And that could so easily have been him and Cody, he realized, if they hadn't washed up here.

Orin finished mending the sapling and they continued walking. Something occurred to him. "I thought you didn't have boats on the island."

"You definitely said that." Cody nodded in

agreement. "I remember everything."

Ferelith paused, uncomfortable. "You're right, it's not exactly true. . . There is always one. Kept by Thao— Well, Nara, actually."

His heart leapt. "Why didn't you say? Could I borrow it?"

She shook her head. "It's kept in a secure boathouse, but there's only one key. And they'll never let you take their only boat. Believe me."

Something in her words made him think that she'd tried.

"I didn't mention Nara's boat because it's not an option."

"But . . . I could at least ask her, and if not, Thao can ask the Eard for a tree for me today." If he managed to get a tree by that afternoon, then he would have two days to make a boat with Cody, then, judging by his journey here, two days to sail home. It might be just enough time.

Ferelith nodded. "He'll be back after harvesting."

Cody patted his leg reassuringly. "We could be lucky and find some wreckage on the east beach."

Eventually the forest ended and they found themselves in a large field of wheat. Insects trilled in the grass. Back in Ironhold, there was one cultivation tower that focused on wheat, but wheat cost a lot of credits, so it wasn't something Orin got to eat often. Here was an enormous, sweeping field of it! Gold-topped, it danced rhythmically in the breeze, whispering a song. *Come dance with us*, it breathed.

Orin wondered: did the crows here ever threaten the crops, as the Engineers had claimed on Ironhold?

Beyond, palm trees were visible down a path to a small beach, azure waves lapping gently across the white sand. It was a warm, clear day, the sort Orin would spend at the top of the cliffs. The sort of day that melted your worries away.

Thinking about it now, they hadn't seen warm, gentle days like this on Ironhold for over a year.

"Wait ... what's that?" he said, pointing ahead. There were places in the wheat that shook a little, as though something was running around inside.

"Wheatenhogs. They tend the wheat and help us collect it."

"What are wheatenhogs?"

Ferelith clicked her tongue on the roof of her mouth and several of the wheatenhogs changed direction and headed their way.

"Are they friendly?" he asked nervously.

"Their teeth are sharp, but they won't bite, not unless you give them reason."

"And what are the reasons?"

She laughed. "Just don't tread on one! Here, you call too – just click your tongue quickly."

He watched her and tried himself.

Suddenly, a small spiny creature emerged from the wheat near their feet. It was around calf height, and a similar golden colour to the wheat, with a pointed snout and ears, prickles the length of its back, and long, almost human-like arms and legs. When Ferelith crouched, clicked her tongue, and put her palms out, it ran into them. Gently, she lifted its cheek a little to reveal razor-sharp teeth. "See, that could have your finger off in one bite."

Orin reared back.

"It's all right, they're just for nibbling the wheat. They can't get enough of it, so they look after it well, watering and caring for it. There's always plenty, and they never mind sharing, do you, little lady?"

The wheatenhog gave several clicks.

"I could help collect with my shear tool?" Cody suggested, opening her arm to reveal the scissor extension.

The wheatenhog clicked a positive trill.

"Excellent, I'm taking that as a yes!" she said, skipping into the field.

After Orin tried the clicking again, several more wheatenhogs emerged from the field. He crouched and found himself folding his fingers into his palms, just in case. "Er, may we have some of your wheat . . . please?"

The wheatenhogs disappeared. Orin thought perhaps he'd got it wrong, but Ferelith nodded at him. A few millidays later, a group of wheatenhogs emerged with great, freshly cut bundles of wheat in their long, spindly arms. Cody arrived, too, with her own bundle.

In no time at all the baskets were full, and Ferelith led Orin and Cody along the path to show them the east side of the island.

They began making their way down the path to the beach, Orin crossing his fingers that the new tide might have washed something in.

But again there was no sign of the boat wreckage.

He looked around, feeling helpless. "What's around the crag? Is there another beach?"

Ferelith gestured at the sun. "It's getting late. You should get back and speak to Thao."

She called for a bog myrtle and helped him and Cody on.

"Aren't you coming?"

Passing him the basket of wheat, she shook her head. "I just remembered I haven't got any offering stones for later."

Something in the sudden flush to her cheeks made Orin doubtful. "We can help?"

"No need, I'll catch up later." And with that, Ferelith patted the bog myrtle and it hurried away, leaving her alone on the beach, and Orin with a strange feeling of suspicion in his chest.

CHAPTER 13

They had only gone as far as the brow of the hill when Orin called to Cody to jump off the bog myrtle. He'd learned to trust his instinct when things were up – sneaking around at the Engineerium had taught him that – and right now there was an uncomfortable feeling in his gut about Ferelith.

"Humans could do with a bit of robot rationality, if you ask me," Cody tutted, brushing herself down. She'd landed with quite an awkward *thud*. "Did you forget I don't have wings any more?"

"Sorry. I think we should go back to the beach."

"Are your circuits working, Orin? Pieces of our boat won't have miraculously washed ashore in the past few millidays."

"Did you think Ferelith was acting strangely?"

"Orin Crowfall, I spend most of my time with you. With that as a benchmark, everything is strange."

"But?"

"But I suppose she does seem more dismissive of you today."

"Exactly." She had been so nice to him the day before, and today she seemed distracted, as if she didn't really want him around. He wanted to know why. "Come on."

They crept back down the hill in the direction Ferelith had taken.

The sky had darkened with a few menacing clouds, and a sudden chill wind charged the hillside. Orin put a finger to his lips and crept on to his knees. Below, he could see Ferelith clambering over rocks at the edge of the beach and out of sight. He scrambled on his elbows to the edge of the crag, but she'd disappeared.

"She's probably just looking for those weird stones, like she said." Cody shrugged. "Come on, we should go back to the village. Thao might have returned."

Orin shook his head. Suspicion had embedded

163

itself and wasn't letting go. "No. If she was looking for stones, why did she want to get rid of us? I'm going down to look. You wait here."

"Er, you don't have a harness and, as I just pointed out via my clumsy exit from the bog myrtle, I have no wings to save you if you fall."

But the feeling in Orin's gut was pulling him over the crag, and before he knew it, he'd swung his body around, found some hand- and footholds, and started edging down the cliff. *Just like West Tip*, he told himself. Soon he heard banging and humming. What was she up to? There was a small, secluded rocky beach below. He couldn't see Ferelith at first, but as he continued down, he spotted her inside a small cave. She was perched on a rock next to a large, arched piece of wood. He recognized the shape, the colours.

It was a large section of their boat!

For a moment he felt elated. It looked like the back end, and much work needed doing, but it was something, and with a bit more wood, it could be fixable. He was about to call her name and scramble down when he realized she had tools laid out and was already repairing it.

This was no accidental discovery. Ferelith must have already known it was here.

Fury fired red-hot in his belly. "Hey!"

When she looked up, the colour drained from her face. She dropped the tool she'd been holding. Half-falling in his urgency, Orin hurried down the remainder of the cliff, then jumped and planted his feet, jabbing an accusing finger at her. "That's my boat!"

"I just found it. Surprise!" She half-grinned awkwardly.

A cold blast of wind looped them. Dark clouds were swarming in from the north.

Orin set his jaw. "And I suppose you happened to already have tools hidden in your basket?"

Her cheeks grew redder. "I ... er ... wasn't sure if I could repair it, so didn't want to get your hopes up."

For a moment he almost believed her, but then he remembered what she'd said yesterday about destiny and being in the wrong box. She wanted to escape from the island too, he realized. She'd pretended to be his friend when really she'd been planning to take his boat for herself the whole time.

Ferelith glanced at the darkening sky. Lightning crackled in the distance.

"You stole it!"

Rain spattered on the rocks, and a cold blast of wind made Ferelith shiver. She wrapped her arms around herself and looked to the ground. "A storm's coming. We need to go back to the village."

"What, and give you a chance to hide my boat again? No way!"

"We'll talk about it back at Heart Tree." She hurriedly packed her tools into her basket and moved to pull the wreckage further up into the cave.

Orin pushed her out of the way. "I'll do that. It's *my* boat." He didn't want her anywhere near it.

"The tide doesn't rise this high, even in a storm. It'll be safe," she said meekly.

He grunted and noticed Cody had also climbed down and was watching from a short distance away. She called out, "This storm means business, Orin! My sensors are going wild. We should get to safety and come back later."

He nodded and waited for Ferelith to leave the cave first, then followed behind, clambering over the rocks back to the east beach. As he scrambled and raindrops started to fall, anger churned inside of him. Ferelith had been the one person he'd thought he could trust in this place. Someone he'd thought was a friend. He'd been wrong about that.

Cody threw him concerned glances. "Even if she did want the boat for herself, at least we found it. We could repair it in a day or two. It'll be smaller but functional."

Ferelith turned but couldn't make eye contact. "We can't call a bog myrtle in a storm. They don't like it. We'll just have to hurry back."

Grudgingly, Orin nodded. He wasn't familiar enough with the island to find the way himself, so he had to follow her. It didn't mean he had to speak to her.

Soon, heavier drops pounded them, and Orin picked Cody up and tucked her inside his jerkin to try and keep her dry. By the time they were back, rain battered them in a relentless torrential cascade. The village was a quagmire of mud and huge, ankle-deep puddles.

Drenched and shivering villagers were bailing water from their trees. Children sobbed and clung to their parents as dark clouds swirled above. In the stormy light the trees were a brilliant green.

A fork of lightning erupted in the sky above and a mighty *boom* vibrated the ground.

Thao, Saviri and Nara ushered all the villagers towards Heart Tree; its massive size provided the best protection. They lit fires, then handed out blankets and warm soup.

Orin huddled with Cody away from the main crowd, wondering how soon he'd be able to get back to his boat. Everyone seemed especially upset by the storm. He thought it was strange – he'd grown used to this kind of weather back on Ironhold. He found himself looking around for Ferelith and saw that she was helping with the soup. *Good*, he told himself. He didn't want to talk to her right now. She had cost him valuable time. He could have been on his way back already. And now the storm was wasting even more time.

A couple of older teenage boys sat watching him and Cody from a short distance away. "Metal freak," one said under his breath, but loud enough that Orin heard it.

"What did you say?" Orin called over. The ball of anger he felt at Ferelith was fighting for an excuse to be unleashed.

The boy shrugged. "We don't want her sort here. It's not natural."

"The Eard shouldn't have let you stay," said the other. "Go back where you came from. You've brought bad luck."

Orin jumped up, but Cody gripped his leg. "Ignore them. They're upset about the storm."

Clenching his hands and releasing them, Orin sat down and looked away.

"Human tempers. Another reason robots are superior." Cody nudged him.

After another deciday or so, the storm abated, and everyone wearily began the clean-up. Orin's anger at Ferelith still seethed, but at least she had the sense to keep away from him.

Dusk fell. Frustrated at the prospect of another day on the island going by without being any closer to getting home, Orin decided to take the opportunity to speak to Thao about getting some wood to help repair the boat. He spotted him talking with Saviri by the fire, so he hovered nearby. He wasn't sure of the right way to approach a leader on Natura. Back home he wouldn't dream of speaking to Commander Forge unless she spoke to him first.

"The storms are getting worse. The Eard is angry. Perhaps some people are missing the ceremonies and we're unaware. I will question every islander and—" Saviri paused and looked to Orin. "Yes?" she said impatiently.

Thao put a hand up. "It's all right. Orin, what can I do for you?"

"I'm sorry, I thought I'd, I mean. . ." His words were coming out jumbled. He was getting it all wrong. He took a breath. "May I speak with you, Thao? Alone."

Saviri cut him a glare sharp as a blade.

"Saviri, I'll think about how we might improve the offering. Go and advise the people about the second cleansing this evening."

Saviri gave a reluctant nod. "Of course, it may otherwise be as some are saying – a matter of bad luck." Her eyes lingered like stone weights on Orin for a moment. Then she left.

Thao indicated for Orin to sit on the rock beside him.

"Sir . . . Thao, I wondered if you might give me permission to gather some wood. It seems some of my boat did wash ashore, and I need to make repairs. Things are happening back home – I need to help my family—" His voice wobbled but he braced himself, needing to be strong. He had to make Thao understand.

Thao stroked his thick beard, troubled.

"Perhaps you could even lend me a boat," Orin continued hopefully. "I'd get it back to you as soon as I could."

The lines on Thao's forehead deepened. "Orin, it is not for me to permit."

"I understand, but Ferelith said you could ask the Eard on my behalf."

"Ferelith asked yesterday about lending you the island boat. I put it to the Eard this morning and it said no."

Orin felt as though he'd reached the edge of a chasm without seeing it was there. What was wrong with these people that they let the Eard decide everything?

He'd have to mend his boat as best he could. It would take a few days, but he still had time. He stood up to leave.

"It's not just the boat." The leader's eyes lost their power and looked weary.

"What do you mean?"

The leaves on the branches above stiffened.

"The Eard has allowed you to stay, but it has also been clear with me on the matter of you leaving."

"Clear?" Creeping realization froze Orin's blood. The air seemed thicker, harder to breathe.

Solemnly, Thao's eyes met his. "The Eard intends you to remain with us. You cannot leave Natura, even if there were a hundred boats."

CHAPTER 14

The next day was blustery, as though the warm winds of the south had decided to fight back against the volatile weather from the north. Despite the blue sky, Orin felt as though a grey film had fallen from the sky and coated the world. After Thao's revelation, Orin had retreated to his sleeping pod with Cody, angry and frustrated. He needed an escape plan.

And yet he'd seen what the Eard did to people who were disobedient. Going against it could cause him even more problems than he already had.

At daybreak, the puddles and sludgy leaves left by the storm made for something good to stomp resentfully through. Cody tottered beside him. "What's the sense in making us stay?" Orin said, pounding onwards.

Cody shrugged. "Perhaps the Eard meant you can't leave until your leg's completely better, and Thao just . . . misinterpreted it?"

Several of the villagers were awake early too and muttered darkly about bad luck under their breaths as Orin passed. It seemed that most of the village had decided the storm was somehow his fault rather than the Eard being angry, as Thao had suggested.

"Orin, wait!"

He stopped and rolled his eyes.

Ferelith.

"I looked for you last night, but you were already asleep."

Cody darted a glance at Orin. Orin had pretended to sleep the previous evening when Ferelith came to his pod. He didn't want to hear her excuses. Perhaps he could have been on his way back to Ironhold by now, if she hadn't hidden his boat. But the worst thing, if he was honest with himself, was that he'd thought they were becoming friends, when really all she'd wanted was to distract him so she could steal his only way of getting home.

"Please, I need to explain."

"All right, I'm listening." He could feel the ball of anger building inside of him.

"You didn't tell Thao, did you? About me, you know—"

He couldn't contain it any longer. "Of course you only care about what Thao thinks – of course you're not actually *sorry*!" he shouted.

Even Cody winced at the force of his words. It wasn't like Orin to be so angry, but he felt so helpless and so far from home.

"I didn't mean it like that, I was about to say—"

Orin cut her off. "Let me see, did I tell Thao about *you* stealing the remains of *my* boat and keeping it secret so that *you* could take it for yourself?" He threw his hands into the air. "For some absurd reason, no, I didn't! Because I thought we were friends, and friends don't stab each other in the back!" He turned away, tense all over. Out of the corner of his eye he heard Cody tut. She didn't approve of what she called "human outbursts".

Ferelith circled to stand in front of him again. "I was about to say, I'm sorry. It wasn't quite like that." She sighed. "Well, it was a bit, but … look, the wreckage washed up on the beach after you arrived. You were ill, and sleeping, so I went back to search and found it hidden in a bank of seaweed. I used a bog myrtle to take it to a more secluded location. I should have told you, I just... You've got to understand, I've wanted this my whole life, since my parents..."

She looked broken, but Orin was still too angry to accept her apology. "I thought I could trust you."

"You can. I really am sorry. I never wanted to... Listen, at first it was easy to take the boat. Then I got to know you a bit more and I wanted to tell you, but I thought you'd think badly of me and—"

"You've got that right."

"And, I was about to say, I had already decided that I was going to tell you about it and help repair it with you, when you found me. I was just thinking of the right way to do it."

"How convenient!" Orin folded his arms.

"I really was! Let me make it up to you, we can go back and repair it together and—"

"I don't want you anywhere near it, or me." He stormed away.

Cody tottered behind him. "You were a little harsh," she said quietly. "I think she was being truthful. She was going to tell you. I'm sophisticated at reading human facial signals, even better than you, it seems."

Ignoring her, Orin trudged onwards to the forest.

Cody sighed and followed him. "That's the thing with you humans. All output sometimes."

He carried on walking, not looking at her. "We're going back to the beach where we came ashore to check if more of the boat has washed up and look for driftwood. The Eard might not allow us to use anything from the island, but it doesn't own the sea."

"And remember," Cody said, hurrying behind, "Ferelith doesn't know the full story, how urgent it is that we get back."

"Cody, the thing with robots is, they never know when to be quiet!"

"Affirmative," she retorted.

On the beach, Orin found a few more small, broken fragments of their boat buried in seaweed and a long, thin branch. His mood began to lift. "Cody, this could be a spear. We need to make something to protect us from the sea monster on the way back."

Cody looked sceptical. "Yes, I'm sure it'll be terrified of a branch, Orin."

Orin gave a frustrated huff. "Look, we've got to work with what we can. You could help, you know. We can sharpen the end. And could you create some sort of sparking device to attach to it, too, to scramble the monster's signal or sever its power supply?"

"Actually, that's not a bad idea. We could repurpose one of my finger tools."

"At the very least we can jab it away, right?" The prospect of facing the mechanical sea monster again filled Orin with ice-cold dread, but they needed to find a way past it if he was going to save his family.

Orin sat on a rock looking out at the waves while Cody used her knife attachment to whittle the end of the branch. Staring out at the sea reminded Orin that home was out there; Mum, Dad, Grandpa were somewhere on that horizon. He rubbed his aching calf. Could he sail with his leg like this? He wasn't sure he had a choice. He shivered.

Cody glanced up at him. "I'll make a small fire."

"I'm fine, just thinking about the journey back."

"And covering up the fact you're still mending.

Human skin is delicate, remember, not like azothe."

In moments, Cody had gathered a small pile of dried seaweed, twigs and shavings. She flipped back a thumb, clicked her fingers and lit a spark. Soon the small fire was glowing, and Orin already felt more positive. He would be able to sail because there was no choice, and he had Cody beside him.

Soon Cody had turned the long branch into a pointed spear. She tapped him. "I still need to create a sparking device in the tip, but how's this as a start?"

Orin nodded. "Not bad."

A frown came over Cody's face.

"I mean, excellent," Orin corrected.

But she wasn't looking at him, she was looking just beyond him. Her eyes widened and she opened her mouth to shout just as everything went dark.

Before Orin could register that his head and shoulders had been covered by some kind of fabric, like a sack, strong arms grabbed him from behind and his hands were swiftly tied behind his back. Yelling and writhing, he was dragged across the sand. Then pain exploded in his leg and he cried out in agony; he'd been kicked in the wound.

Cold water enveloped his legs; he was being

dragged into the waves. His heart hammered against his ribs. "Stop, please," he begged. Where was Cody? Were they doing the same to her too? Fear gnawed his gut. "Don't hurt her!"

"Go back to the sea, and take your bad luck with you," a male voice said.

With a lurch, Orin fell forward and was enveloped in cold wet. His lungs gasped for air and instead he gulped in acrid saltwater. He thrashed and writhed, but he couldn't get up. There was a weight on his back. Furiously, he fought to get out from under it. Momentarily, he surfaced, choked and spluttered, then was pushed down again, dragged further out, and with everything he had he tried to get up. His hand erupted with a burning pain; he must have scraped against a rock or something. The water was in his mouth, and his lungs convulsed. This was it. He was going to drown. All felt hopeless; he'd survived the mechanical sea monster, and now he was going to die, far from home.

Then the pressure pushing him down suddenly relented, and he flailed in the water, trying to get above but falling beneath the waves, his legs weak and muscles spent. Then someone grabbed him and he was yanked upwards. Vomiting up water, his lungs felt bruised, but he took a hungry gulp of air in case he was pushed under again, then writhed and twisted against the hands on him. A voice cut through.

"Orin! It's me, you're safe." Someone pulled off the sack.

Ferelith. She unbound the rope from his wrists.

Exhaustion, pain and relief shook Orin's limbs. Turning, he saw two figures running back up the beach – he recognized them as the older teens from the village who had goaded him and Cody during the storm.

Ferelith's hands trembled and she clenched them. "Orin, I'm so sorry. I should've been here."

Orin looked frantically around in the waves for Cody, his heart frozen in his chest. She was nowhere to be seen.

"She's still on the beach. Come on." Ferelith pointed at a moving heap of cloth back on the shore, and Orin exhaled with relief. As Ferelith put an arm around him and they staggered back out of the water, Cody managed to cut herself free, her fierce round eyes softening as she saw Orin and Ferelith.

They all sat on the sand together, panting. "You … took on … those two … on your own, Ferelith?" He clenched his hand to his chest where it burned, and tried to ignore the throb in his leg, but at least he was alive.

"Yeah." She shrugged. "That's just Blaine and Attica, they're actually pretty gutless." She rubbed a sore-looking patch on her cheek. The wooden spear Cody had been carving wasn't far away. "I'm glad that was to hand. Someone's head is going to hurt for a while."

Cody smirked. "Good."

They found themselves laughing, despite the horror of what had just happened.

Then Orin remembered he was meant to be annoyed with Ferelith.

"Just throwing it out there, but perhaps now's a good time to forgive people," Cody said out of the corner of her mouth.

Looking across at Ferelith, he knew what Cody had been trying to tell him earlier was true. He gave a small nod. "OK, I guess after that I kind of have to forgive you."

Her face lit up. "Really? I really *am* sorry I took

your boat. I wouldn't have abandoned you. I just didn't want you to mend it and disappear without me, not without getting to know me a bit so that, perhaps. . ." She hesitated.

"What?" he asked curiously.

"I was hoping that maybe... Well, I wondered if . . . maybe . . . I could go with you?"

Orin and Cody exchanged a glance. Why anyone would choose to go to Ironhold to face what they had to face was beyond them. But he remembered he hadn't explained what was going on back home. He looked to Cody, who nodded. "There are some things I need to tell you first."

As they sat looking at the sea, he told Ferelith everything: from the moment he first saw Commander Forge steal the Eard's life-light, to being caught listening in on the Core's secret plans for human evolution, and his desperate flight from Ironhold.

"So, I totally get it if you'd rather not come with us," he finished.

Ferelith didn't say anything for a long time. Orin wondered whether she'd change her mind about coming now, and found he'd feel disappointed if she did. He liked the idea of her at his side as they set out again.

"Islands with ancient Eards are carefully balanced ecosystems built up over hundreds of years. If you kill an Eard suddenly, then everything on the island will die too," she said at last.

He nodded. "I didn't know that until I heard Commander Forge talking about her plans. That's why I need to get home. I have to get my family out of there."

They sat, staring out at the water, for another long stretch of silence, until Ferelith turned her head towards him. "Your leg's bleeding again. You obviously need me with you . . . you know, to patch you up and keep an extra eye out."

Warmth glowed in his chest. The thought of the three of them heading to Ironhold together made it all seem more possible. Like they really had a chance. "We'll be glad to have you with us. And my leg will be fine; I'm just glad to be alive." He relived the attack in his mind again, and his stomach turned to think of how it could've ended. "Thank you for saving me." He paused; something occurred to him. "Those boys were willing to go against the Eard?"

Ferelith nodded. "They probably thought they

could get away with it, here on the outskirts of the island. And they didn't count on me turning up."

Somewhere behind, the bushes rustled. Orin jumped up, half-expecting to see the boys back to try again, but it was Nara who emerged from the undergrowth.

Ferelith's eyes widened. "How long have you been there?"

Nara glared at Ferelith with thin, suspicious eyes and folded her arms. "Long enough."

CHAPTER 15

Nara had Ferelith's hands bound. As they made their way through the forest, Orin considered running, but he couldn't abandon Ferelith, not after she'd saved him. Hurriedly, Ferelith told Nara about the boys who had attacked, and Orin guessed she was trying to divert Nara's attention from what she'd just overheard.

"I'll make sure they are dealt with," Nara replied. "But *you* need to stop all these foolish thoughts of leaving. I'm taking you back to my father." Then she glared at Orin. "Why the Eard wants you to stay, I have no idea, but you're coming with us too."

Orin held up his hands defensively. After what had just happened, he didn't have the strength to fight, but his heart sank at the thought of being trapped in a thorny prison or being stuck with the bind. He darted a glance at Cody. Perhaps she could sneak off now, and rescue him if they did imprison him? Nara caught him looking.

She narrowed her eyes. "You'd better not try anything funny either."

As Nara escorted them through the village, they began to draw attention from villagers going about their business. Nara summoned Thao and Saviri at Heart Tree and sent someone to find the two boys who had attacked Orin.

Nara talked at length with Thao and Saviri. Thao kept glancing over, the furrows of worry deepening as Nara spoke.

Blaine and Attica were marched back to Heart Tree, both looking shamefaced and anxious.

Well, it serves them right, Orin thought bitterly.

Word seemed to have spread like fire through dry wood, and the people of the village stopped what they were doing and hurried over to watch. Whispers rippled through the crowd and the atmosphere grew increasingly tense.

Thao cast a solemn glance Blaine and Attica's

way before approaching the tree and putting his hands to the roots.

"What's he doing?" Orin whispered to Ferelith.

"Communicating with the Eard."

Fronds began growing up from the earth beside the two boys. They looked down, stunned, then exchanged a look of alarm. "But we were doing it for the Eard!" called Blaine. "The boy brought us bad luck!"

"Silence!" said Saviri. "Only the Eard decides what is right."

The fronds extended and snaked around the boys' ankles and lower legs, then tightened, gripping them. The boys looked at each other, beads of sweat forming on their foreheads. Suddenly, Attica cried out, and Blaine fell to the ground, the boys' muscles turning rigid. There were gasps in the crowd.

Tiny specks of silvery light sparked in the roots that gripped the boys' calves and ankles.

"Father?" Nara asked, turning to him. The villagers' eyes were wide with alarm.

"The Eard decides on the punishment," said Thao, but Orin thought that his usually strong voice carried a note of unease.

A sick feeling churned inside of Orin as he watched, mesmerized. The silvery light and the way it moved looked very similar to something he'd seen before, back when Commander Forge had extracted life-light from the Eard of Ironhold.

As the roots grew tauter and the lights grew brighter, a strange, distant look came over the boys' eyes.

"What is it doing?" Orin whispered.

Ferelith's voice trembled. "I don't know. This is worse than the bind. I've never seen the Eard do this."

"It's ... like what Commander Forge did on Ironhold, only ... in reverse."

Ferelith looked at him, horrified. "You mean, it's taking their souls?"

Orin stepped forward and yelled, "Stop it!"

The Eard seemed to relax its grip slightly and the boys blinked, as though awakening from a troubled sleep. The light had stopped flowing but the bind remained.

The crowd was utterly silent, a mixture of shock and fear on everyone's faces. The Eard was all-powerful and no one was about to stand up to it.

Orin turned back to Ferelith and panic-whispered, "It's not going to do that to you, is it?"

The colour drained from Ferelith's face. "No. It'll likely be a tree prison for a while. I'll be fine."

But Orin saw her throat constrict as she swallowed. She was scared.

"The boy was intending to leave against the wishes of the Eard!" Saviri suddenly shouted. "If the Eard will punish Ferelith, it should punish him too!"

Thao extended his hands in a pleading motion. "We will keep a close eye on both of them from now on. Enough punishment has been carried out for one day."

But the Eard had its own plans.

Like a pair of lassos, it whipped out two vines and took hold of Orin's and Ferelith's ankles, launching the pair into the air to hang upside down. Orin's stomach turned and his limbs jolted painfully. New vines lashed in from all angles, joining, fusing, snatching, gripping their wrists.

Somewhere below, Thao and Nara cried out for the Eard to stop, that it was going too far. Even Saviri looked aghast.

Orin and Ferelith were like two flies caught in

an enormous spider-web prison. Bound tightly, Orin could barely move a muscle, and every part of him felt painfully stretched.

Trees rustled in the distance. A dark shape was passed from branch to branch. Something was being brought towards them. As it neared, Orin realized it was the remains of their boat that had been on the east beach. The Eard was carrying it to Heart Tree. It brought the boat before them, wrapped it tightly with a large vine, and with a squeeze, the structure exploded into a thousand tiny shards of wood.

Nara called out in horror and Orin saw Thao draw her close.

Terrified eyes looked up from the village. Then various people broke off from the crowd and began running for their cleansing bowls, laying stones and muttering prayers.

Everyone seemed to have forgotten Cody, who had tucked herself behind a bush and was staring up at Orin. Struggling to move his wrist, Orin just managed to get his thumb and fingers to connect and make a clicking motion. He could only hope that Cody understood.

She did, because she mouthed, "You've got to be kidding."

He shook his head as much as he could get it to move.

In an instant, Cody was by the web. Flipping back a thumb, she clicked her fingers and an electrical spark lit. She jabbed it into the Eard.

The web flashed as electrical current flowed through it, and an uncomfortable tingle radiated through Orin. But it did as he'd hoped. The web loosened, and he and Ferelith fell to the ground.

Clouds swarmed above and daylight was snuffed out like an extinguished flame. The light deepened, almost to night, around them. Silence fell as everyone took in the shock of what had happened. Like braced arrows, all eyes of the village set on Orin and Ferelith.

Then a deep vibration rocked the earth, followed by what Orin could only describe as a growl, a noise so deep and visceral that it rocked every cell in his body.

They both jumped to their feet.

"What's happening?" Orin said.

"I think we just made it really angry," Ferelith breathed.

She was right. Like the heightened coursing of

his own blood, Orin could sense the Eard's fury. Its power made his skin prickle with fear, but Orin had to do everything he could to get away.

"Can you get us to Nara's boat in the dark?"

"It's locked away!"

"We'll work it out when we get there."

An icy wind wrapped itself around them like a snake. Again the ground howled a foreboding challenge.

Ferelith pushed Orin forward. "We need to go. Now!"

Scooping up Cody, Orin started running.

"Follow me!" Ferelith shouted. "Move unpredictably in a zigzag so the Eard has less chance to grab us!"

The ground shook again, and they dodged from side to side, past falling branches and jumping over flailing, angry vines.

As they neared the village perimeter, they skidded to a halt. The statue tree before them creaked like snapping wood and bore down over them. Roots ripped from the ground.

"I thought these things didn't move!" said Orin, panicked.

Cody gripped Orin's neck. "I guess the Eard is pretty angry."

With a yank of his arm, Ferelith pulled them on into the forest. "We have to outrun it!"

Anger throbbed in the air. Earth-shattering footsteps pursued them as leaves and wood debris rained down. Muffled screams caught on the wind, and Orin, running as fast he could, was unsure if they belonged to the distant villagers or if they were their own.

Somehow, the edge of the outer forest came into view, the wheat field beyond lit by moonlight. Orin and Ferelith fought their way through the undergrowth, stumbling and staggering to try and make it past the final trees, but they seemed to thicken and tighten around them. Branches swung menacingly towards them as they lurched and fought past.

Orin crouched, ready to spring, as vines whipped at him. "Hold tight to my neck, Cody!" He reached for Ferelith. "Jump up!" Then, "Dive down!" they yelled between them as the vines came relentlessly from all angles.

But the vines weren't only whipping, they were

twisting together before them; it was becoming harder to make their way through the final part of the forest. Orin gripped Ferelith's hand. If they were split up, he knew he didn't stand a chance. She knew the island inside out, whereas he would easily get lost in the deepening gloom.

"This way!" Ferelith shouted.

They blundered through the bracken. The roar of the wind was deafening. Somewhere above the trees, the sky darkened further, blocking any moonlight.

Breath heaving in the chill, their legs on fire, Orin and Ferelith somehow emerged on to the east path, the vastness of the sea suddenly visible before them. Only the wheat field stood between them and the beach now.

"Come on!" Ferelith called, but as they approached, a cracking sound split the air. Like rapidly freezing ice, the wheat became blackened struts, stiff and sharp as spears.

Orin cried out as he caught one and it cut into his flesh. "Are you all right?" he called to Cody, whose arms were round his neck, her head buried in his shoulder.

"I think under the circumstances, we could all be doing better!"

They turned and ran back in the other direction, but the trees were in a frenzy and Orin couldn't believe they'd made it through in the first place.

"We'll have to skirt the field on the cliff path," Ferelith called, and without giving him a chance to respond, she started running towards it. The ground rumbled and rocks bounced and tumbled.

A dark shape became visible below. "Down there. The boathouse!" Ferelith called.

With a crack, the cliff path before them fell away and they lurched back to a standstill. The only route left was up through the wooded slope and down to the bay. Ferelith pointed to where it looked clearest. They ran back along the clifftop path, but they would have to go through the final patch of forest on the slope.

With an almighty *creak*, a tree ripped from its roots, fell, and hurtled towards them. They jumped out of the way, but more were falling. They wobbled and pitched around the rolling trees, made it up the slope, and were almost through when the largest tree tore itself from its roots and began falling straight for them. Orin hurled himself aside, his hand ripping from Ferelith's. The tree crashed down in a flurry of flailing branches, scratching and tearing at his clothes and skin. A large branch thwacked his chest and sent him flying back and Cody clattering away. His face distorted with pain, and he felt frantically for Cody, who shouted that she was fine.

"Ferelith?" he groaned. Where was she? He hadn't seen her since they'd been torn apart. Could the full force of the tree have hit her?

Everything fell into a sudden, unexpected quiet. Even the wind seemed to pause.

The glimmer of Cody's silvery azothe shone through the leaves a short distance away. "Cody, can you see Ferelith?"

"No."

Somehow, Orin clambered out of the grip of the branch. Chest heaving with dread, he looked around frantically.

But all was silent.

CHAPTER 16

Grappling through the thicket, Orin's hands met the wide trunk of the fallen tree. He prayed they wouldn't meet flesh too.

"Ferelith?" He ripped at the twigs and leaves, searching.

There was no reply. No sign of her.

"She's not over here," called Cody.

Nervously Orin continued to look around the tree. Nothing would survive the full weight of it.

Clambering over the trunk, he heard a cough, so quiet he almost missed it.

"Ferelith!"

"I'm here!"

She was alive! She must have managed to jump

out of the way too. Relief loosened the vice-grip of dread that had held him, but anger at the Eard boiled his blood.

"Are you done now? Are you?" he yelled furiously.

But it wasn't done.

As Orin made his way towards where he had heard Ferelith's voice, vines snaked their way around his body. Growling with frustration, he tugged at them. Swiftly, they encircled Cody's hands, binding around and around so that she couldn't release any of her tools. They were immobile, but still the vegetation kept wrapping them both. The Eard's grip tightened, making Orin gasp for air. After everything that had happened, it couldn't be over.

"Orin, I'm bound like a bobbin – I can't release a thing. *Do* something!" Cody called out.

"What exactly do you want me to do, Cody?" As if in response, the vines tightened further around his chest. The edges of Orin's vision blurred.

"Orin, it's all down to you. If you don't do something now, it's all over."

Orin tried again to rip himself free, to gasp for breath. If only he could make the Eard understand why he had to get back. That his family needed help, that he *had* to get home. If he didn't—

Wait. Could he at least try to talk to it? He didn't have a mark, but neither did Thao. It didn't matter; he had to try, and just hope it would listen.

Squirming, he just wriggled a hand free and put it to the vine wrapping his chest. He tried to clear his mind, and then suddenly felt hot, electric prickles pulsating on his palm . . . and for a moment he felt as though he were flying. He heard a voice somewhere inside of him; not human, it was a sound filled with echoes, layered with ethereal tones as light as starlight alongside rich, earthy bass notes.

We must protect ourselves. Long have we existed. I see the suffering of your Eard, I feel what is happening.

A rush of emotions and images flooded Orin, like a dream, except he was neither asleep nor awake. He saw people building, the conservatory being constructed over the Eard of Ironhold, and a feeling of sadness swamped him. Then he saw Commander Forge draining the life-light; he felt the anger of the Eard of Natura to see this, as though it was his own life-light. He watched the roots blacken and die, the pain stabbing him like a scythe to the heart.

"You know," Orin breathed.

The Eards are life. We are the link. You cannot hurt one of us without hurting all.

Images of the terrible storms of Ironhold flew through his mind.

The balance is weakening. It must not happen here too.

The Eards were connected. It could see and feel everything Commander Forge had done.

People must learn. They must feel the hurt it feels. They must understand.

The reason the Eard of Natura was so controlling was suddenly clear: it was afraid. It couldn't help the Eard of Ironhold, but it could prevent the same thing from happening here. It had been controlling the people, growing increasingly cruel because it was scared. And the people of Natura had let it, so it got worse and worse.

An image of himself at the trial flashed into his mind. The Eard had wanted him to stay, to save him from Ironhold's fate.

You must not go back.

But there was his family and everyone else on Ironhold. He had to show the Eard of Natura another side; that not everyone there was bad. They just didn't know what the Eard should be – they didn't know what Commander Forge was doing to it. He needed to show the Eard the goodness he intended to save. Focusing hard, he pictured the sun streaming through the window in West Tip, with him sitting on Grandpa's knee singing silly songs while Grandpa twiddled his moustache into curls and made Orin giggle. Then Dad baking, laughing with Mum when she taught him how to mend the generator; Grandma's book; Mum and Dad hugging him tightly; Grandpa joking with his friends at their weekly knitting meet-ups; the green-caped cultivators carefully nurturing their crops in the towers; the grey-cloaked engineers mending the fixies to help; medi-bots flying in to assist Mum when she fell in a storm.

"There are good people and good things in Ironhold. They are worth saving. Let me go back to try and stop the Core. Let me help the others. Let me try to save the Eard."

The Eard of Natura was wavering, but Orin could sense that it wasn't enough. He had to shock it into realizing its behaviour was wrong … because …

because just like Vida Forge was convinced that her intentions were for the greater good, so was the Eard. In Forge's eyes, she was behaving in a rational way. The people of Ironhold and its Eard had become a disposable part of the natural evolution, but the thousands of Ironholders would certainly think differently when they knew. What sort of life was one where only a few mattered? The Eard of Natura was rational in its belief too. It was controlling the people to protect them and itself, but it was wrong. It was hurting them.

"You think controlling the people and making them do all these rituals is the only way. You've even got them collecting silly black stones, for no purpose at all just because they think it makes you happy, but you're only doing it to dominate them. You're behaving just like Forge," said Orin. "Don't you see? In trying to protect yourself from people like her, you've started to become an oppressor, just like she is controlling the Eard of Ironhold!"

Everything on Natura seemed to pause. With a blaze of light, the sky erupted with lightning and a boom of thunder that shook Orin's very soul. Wind rushed and spiralled around him so that everything blurred. This was it; he'd really angered the Eard now!

And then. . .

Silence. Orin could feel the cold realization of the comparison sinking in to the Eard, this amazing beautiful, powerful, sentient creature, at danger of becoming like the worst of humans.

The voice of the Eard sang inside of him.

You are right, Orin. I could not see, but . . . you are right.

The wind abated, thunder ceased, clouds lightened, and the vines loosened and eventually shrank out of the way.

It had worked! The Eard of Natura had heard him. It finally understood!

Go, Orin Crowfall.

He called for Ferelith, who emerged, groaning, from the leaves.

Extending a hand, he helped her to standing.

She brushed debris off her clothes. "What happened? Why did everything stop?"

"I . . . communicated with it." He looked at his hands, still amazed. He'd actually formed a connection. Feelings churned in his belly: happiness that Ferelith was all right; pride that he'd achieved something that felt important, that they could now head to Ironhold; but also trepidation in the knowledge that it was far from over and there was a momentous task ahead.

Ferelith pulled a large twig from Orin's hair.

Cody crawled out from the bushes.

"It can sense what's going on in Ironhold. It's known everything this whole time. That's why it didn't want me to leave. But it listened; it understood it has to let us go, not only to give us a chance to save the people, but because it could see that it too was becoming an oppressor, like Forge." Orin still couldn't believe what had just happened.

Cody looked at him like a proud parent.

"What?" he said.

"Nothing," she replied with a small smile.

They continued down to the boathouse.

As they approached the shoreline, he heard a shout. He turned to see Nara running towards them and his heart sank. Her scowl was fierce.

"You can't stop us!" Orin called. "We have to go, Nara. Even the Eard sees that now."

Ferelith folded her arms and shook her head. "We're leaving, Nara! Just go."

Nara was close enough now that they could see her roll her eyes. "You really think you can sail blindly into the horizon and combat the mechanical sea monster?"

"You know about that?" said Orin suspiciously.

"Of course." She flicked her braid over her shoulder. "I've sailed these waters with my mother ever since I could walk. I've seen that thing loads of times."

"What?" Ferelith asked, astounded. "Why did you never tell me?"

"Because, knowing you, you would have sneaked off in a boat to try to get a glimpse for yourself! It's too dangerous to go off like this."

Orin couldn't let her stop them. "Nara, there's no time to explain, but back on Ironhold, things are about to get really bad – bad as in thousands could die. I'm the only one who knows they're in danger, and if I don't make it back, then I will have failed them."

"It's true," said Ferelith. "We *have* to go."

Nara's expression was unreadable. "That may be,

but if you die on the way, what good will that do? What's your plan for getting past the sea monster?"

"We had a spear. At least we were making one when you interrupted us on the beach earlier." He had to make her see. Looking her square in the eyes, he said, "Imagine if Thao and Saviri were in the same situation. You'd do anything to help them, I know you would. I need to make it back to Ironhold to save my family."

After looking up to the sky for a moment, Nara returned his steely glare. "Ferelith is my cousin. I have to protect her too."

"We *will* find a way."

After a moment of thought, Nara took a breath. "You're not going—"

"Just try and stop us," snapped Ferelith.

"Yeah, you can't stop us," added Cody, whizzing one of her finger screwdrivers at her.

"If you would listen, you'd know I was about to say that you're not going . . . without a bit of help from me."

"What?" Orin and Ferelith said in tandem.

"You're right. I would cross all the oceans of this world for my family. I would stop anyone in my way.

And I . . . I didn't think the Eard would do what it did. It went too far. I'm sorry, Ferelith."

"It's all right, cousin. We're fine. But there is one thing you can do to make it up."

"My boat?" She grinned. "You were about to find a way to break in and take it anyway." She took a chain with a key on it from around her neck. "Here, you can have it. There are maps and supplies already inside the boat. The Eard seems calmer now. You should hurry before it realizes what you're doing and tries to stop you."

Ferelith rushed to open the boathouse with Cody, while Orin held back a moment.

"The Eard let me communicate with it back in the trees. It's been so scared of us humans messing things up, that's why it's become so harsh. It knew all about the problems on Ironhold. It listened to me, and it knows we have to get back, so it's giving us a chance to do something."

Nara frowned in thought. "Well, maybe there is more to you than being washed-up flotsam." She kicked at a pebble by her feet. "Look after my cousin, Orin Crowfall."

"We'll look out for each other."

Inside the boathouse, the boat rested on a wheeled platform. Together, all four pulled it through the doors and down the beach a short way.

Her face glowing but her eyes glistening, Ferelith rushed over and pulled Nara into a hug. "Thank you."

After a moment, Nara pulled away and quickly wiped her own tears. "Just promise me you'll stay safe."

Ferelith nodded.

Orin lifted Cody inside the boat and scrambled in after her. Then Nara and Ferelith pushed the platform silently out into the sea, where the boat bobbed in the waves and floated up from its rolling base. Orin pulled Ferelith up over the side.

It was time to go.

CHAPTER 17

The boat was sturdier than the one Orin and Cody had arrived in, with double sails and even a small cabin for shelter. There were maps, food supplies, and even a big tank of water. As they drifted further out to sea, the three of them studied the maps by the light of Cody's finger torch. Ironhold wasn't marked on there, but Orin recognized a couple of features from his original journey. For the first time in days, he felt like he was making real progress. Finally, finally they were on their way.

He just hoped they wouldn't be too late.

"Those arches look like the sea rock forest where we crashed, so if we find them in the west, then arc to the north, we should find the place where the seas meet."

They sifted through a chest filled with navigation equipment.

"What's this thing?" said Ferelith, holding up a triangular instrument and pulling it in and out like a metal beak.

Orin shrugged. "And what are these for? They look like pincers, or maybe they're for pointing?" He jabbed them in the direction of the moon.

"Look, this one spins!" Ferelith whirled a small arrow on a round tool.

With a loud tut, Cody took the equipment from them. "No offence, but it's far more likely my superior robotic brain will figure them out. Orin, you're probably the most experienced sailor, so you take the sails. Ferelith, you figure out what we might use as a weapon against the mechanical sea monster."

Soon Natura was a dark dot melding into the horizon, and they had all settled into their tasks.

The night was quiet as a whisper. Cody managed to make sense of some star charts in the store and Ferelith fashioned some spare oars into a new spear. They calculated that they would reach the rock forest by dawn. But after a deciday or so, they were exhausted, and Orin didn't want to risk crashing into the rocky arches again, so they decided to drop anchor and get some sleep.

At first light, Orin set sail again. Ferelith navigated, while Cody cooked a breakfast of nutty porridge and dried fruit. By Orin's calculation it was now six days since he'd left Ironhold, which meant there were only four days before Commander Forge would put her plan into action. And that was only if nothing had changed in his absence, he thought uneasily.

The day was grey and increasingly menacing as they progressed west. After half a deciday of sailing, the great curving rocks criss-crossing out of the water came into sight. A shiver ran the length of Orin's spine when he thought back to being smashed about by the mechanical sea monster.

But the nearer they were, the darker the day became. Behind the structures, stretching across the northern horizon, was a thick, looming bank of cloud. The water was becoming increasingly choppy. Ferelith clutched the side of the boat.

"Are you all right?" Orin noticed she'd turned

sickly pale as the waves became rougher.

She put a hand up and swallowed. "Fine, I just don't like this . . . churning."

Orin tried to position the boat so it pointed into the waves, to minimize the rolling sensation, but the juddering bounce of the waves was becoming relentless.

Cody joined Orin at the sails. "That's no ordinary sea mist. Look at the way it's moving. It's turning within itself, almost as though it has no intention of going anywhere."

Light sparked within the cloud and it rumbled with a roar like vengeful laughter.

"I don't like the thought of sailing into that!" Orin said.

Cody did a quick calculation. "In fine weather, it would take us a full day to get there, if we carry on northwards."

The weather to the north was anything but fine.

Orin squinted. "Perhaps we should wait and see if it passes."

"Excellent idea," called Ferelith, who was leaning over the side of the boat, having been sick. "And maybe we could retreat to the calmer waters until then."

As they waited through the morning, frustration fizzled in Orin's chest, his eyes barely leaving the horizon as he hoped for a change in the perpetual storm.

Cody tapped his shoulder. "My readings are detecting that the storm still isn't shifting. What if it's been there since we first came this way?"

"That's not helpful, Cody."

"But it is possible."

Emerging from the cabin, Ferelith passed Orin a handful of nuts and seeds. "What do we do?"

"What can we do, apart from wait for a break, or take a risk and go straight through it?"

"That's not taking a risk, that's certain death," said Cody.

"Let me know when you've come up with a better idea, Miss Logic!"

Ferelith unrolled a map out on the deck. "When you two have finished bickering, I actually have an idea." She drew her finger over the map and tapped it. "We need to go back."

"What?" Orin couldn't believe what he was hearing. "If that's the best you've got, you can keep your ideas to yourself."

"I don't mean to Natura; I mean we head back east, then we arc around the storm, past this island here and whatever this is here, and approach Ironhold from the north-east side."

The dark clouds swirled and growled in the distance as though daring them to try and come any closer.

"It's not a bad suggestion," said Cody. "We're not even going to be able to see the mechanical sea monster, let alone spear it, if we head into that."

Orin felt his skin prickle at the thought of facing the monster again. "How much time will we lose?"

With a shrug, Cody said, "I can't be sure, but judging by how far we've come, and depending on how far the storm stretches, I'd estimate three more days."

"Including today?"

"Excluding today. But I'm being cautious with my calculations."

"That would mean arriving back nine days after we left." Commander Forge and the engineers were planning to finish off the Eard and abandon Ironhold on the tenth day. It was going to be tight.

"It's your call, Orin," Ferelith said. "If we wait here for another day to see if the storm fades, and it doesn't, we lose our option of arcing east."

She was right. They couldn't waste any more time hesitating, and although the words made his heart twist, he said, "All right. Let's head east."

CHAPTER 18

The further east they sailed, the milder the weather became again, allowing them to make good progress. Even though the route was now frustratingly longer, it was certainly safer. As they travelled on, the natural curvature of the horizon hid the storm from view, so Cody used her sensors to detect the status of the storm and confirmed it was still raging in the northern seas.

Ferelith had returned to her brighter self now the waves were calmer, and she was constantly rushing eagerly to the edges of the boat, pointing out every new thing she saw.

"Look at this! It's so beautiful! What do you think it is?"

Orin passed the sail rope to Cody and joined Ferelith to look over the edge. The sea was the most beautiful, translucent aqua-blue, and the seabed was visible a short distance below. Colours exploded in flower shapes and branches: orange, lime, deep purple, mustard yellow, cerise.

A memory of being in a boat with Grandma erupted in Orin's mind. "It's a coral reef! We used to have one not far from Ironhold." It was strange: he'd never recalled this memory until now, but the sight of the coral fired something in his brain. He must have only been a toddler, but he could remember Grandma pointing out the coral to him. She had shown him where it was bleaching, turning to white bones beneath the water.

"Used to?" Ferelith asked.

He frowned. "Yes, something killed it. I remember my grandma showing me the coral. It was dying, and Grandma said we were going to find a way to save it. But it's all dead now." Could the coral have been somehow connected to the Eard of Ironhold?

Cody threw him a knowing glance. "I can see where your obsession with saving plants might have started."

"Makes sense," said Ferelith, smiling.

"Human family traits are a curious thing. Fixies are programmed to repair things, yet your human programming must somewhere be telling you not to pass a snapped twig without trying to mend it."

Orin raised his eyebrows. "Thank you for your analysis, professor. But perhaps me and Grandma both happen to just like plants." He gave Cody a soft tap on the nose.

They sailed onwards into the east, over the great reef, until the sun sank into a burning pool of light on the western horizon.

Cody perched on the bow. "It should be safe to turn north now."

"Maybe we should drop anchor while the water is still shallow," suggested Ferelith. "If the map is accurate, we should be reaching something marked *the silver beneath* soon. We could spend the night there."

Home still felt very far away, but Orin knew that resting for the night was the right thing to do. They couldn't afford to accidentally navigate the wrong way in the dark.

They continued further east, Orin at the sails, Cody keeping a check on the weather and Ferelith gazing over the side of the boat, searching for something silver. All of a sudden, she shouted, "Look!"

Sure enough, beneath the waves was an enormous silver dome shape.

"Hey, it's like the one we saw on our journey to Natura. Look, Cody!"

"It's so beautiful. What is it?" Ferelith breathed, eyes wide.

Orin sat on the edge of the boat watching a strange, many-tentacled creature swim past. "This is going to sound unreal, but in my grandma's book she wrote a story about islands coming from the sky thousands of years ago."

"From up there?" Ferelith paused, looking up at darkening sky . . . then burst out laughing.

Orin set his teeth and wished he hadn't said anything.

She pushed his shoulder. "I'm not laughing at *you*! It's just such an incredible thought, don't you think? An island falling from the sky!"

It *was* an incredible thought.

"Who do you think brought it here?"

"Maybe we'll never know."

The light of curiosity shone in Ferelith's eyes. "Perhaps one day we could dive down and investigate; you know, when we don't have a ticking time bomb hanging over us. When we can sail the world free and easy."

Orin smiled to himself, imagining how wonderful that would be. The time and freedom to document all the amazing plants and animals. To learn more about how they all lived together. He could search the world for the crows, instead of waiting for them to appear on the horizon.

In the little amount of daylight left, they watched a large shoal of silvery fish dart and dance below, then decided to drop the anchor, get some sleep, and make an early start.

Their aim the next day was to reach a small island marked on the map simply as "island". Their water supply was beginning to run low and they hoped to be able to refill the tank and maybe get some more food supplies.

It was a fine sailing day. Orin could almost believe they were simply three young adventurers exploring the world without a care. There were moments, when he held the sail ropes and felt the wind in his hair, with the beauty of the wide blue all around, that he felt truly free, as though anything was possible.

Then he would remember the reality of Ironhold and the task ahead, and it brought him back down with a crash.

Cody trundled over with a cup of water. "Here, I'm rationing your water." She narrowed her eyes. "I know that expression on your face, Orin Crowfall."

"Do you?"

"Yes, the one where you think everything is hopeless and you're just a boy from West Tip, so what can *you* do."

"I—"

But he didn't get a chance to finish because Ferelith jumped in. "Hey, you both need to look at this. This is really strange." She turned the map around in her hands.

"What?"

"Look, over there!" She pointed to the east. "Do you see that? There's an island over there, but according to where I *think* we are, it's not in the right place. At least it's not the island we're looking for."

Orin shrugged. "Maybe it's been marked wrong on the map."

"We should head there," said Cody. "In case it *is* the island we want. We're getting low on water. You humans need liquids or you perish very swiftly."

"But if it's not the island on the map, then we'll waste precious time by stopping."

Ferelith shrugged. "You're captain, Orin. It's your call."

"Am I?" He blushed. Despite everything, he wasn't sure a mere server from West Tip could be a captain.

"Don't let it go to your head, I'm going to captain the next trip." Ferelith smiled.

"I don't think we need to worry about making a decision," said Cody.

They both looked at her, confused. "Why?"

"Because the island appears to be moving closer to *us*."

Squinting into the distance, they saw with some alarm that she was right.

"Maybe the current changed without us realizing, and it's pulling us towards it?" Orin suggested.

Cody leant over the edge of the boat, a finger

sensor dangling in the water. "The current isn't going in that direction. It doesn't make sense. The only logical answer is that the island is moving."

"How can an island move?" Orin and Ferelith stared at each other, having spoken the same words. With every moment it was getting closer.

"What can you see, Cody? Is it dangerous?" asked Orin.

"Rocks, trees, nothing out of the ordinary."

"I think we should check it out," said Ferelith.

"Really, you want to take that risk? Wait, you said I'm captain, so—"

Cody coughed. "Argue all you want, but at the rate it's moving, it's going to catch up with us and there's nothing we can do about it."

CHAPTER 19

As it neared, the island slowed. It was a great dome of an island with mottled brown rocks.

Then something extraordinary happened. Another, smaller dome rose from beneath the water. Orin, Ferelith and Cody stared as two massive eyes blinked at them and nostrils opened wide.

An icy chill ran down Orin's neck, and his arms prickled with fear. "It's a monster!" They'd avoided the storm only to run into this. He looked about desperately for anything that might help them.

Ferelith pulled him back. "It's not a monster. I know these creatures; they come to the south beach of Natura sometimes, though nothing like this size. Look at its great fins underwater."

The creature stopped when it was only the length of the boat away and stared benignly at them.

"It's a giant turtle. Utterly harmless. But a thousand times bigger than any I've ever seen!" Ferelith smiled. "It's a turtle island! I think it must have wanted to say hello."

"And it has trees growing on its back." Orin gaped.

"Look at this!" called Cody, pointing to the water. Thousands of yellow fish swam alongside the turtle, chomping algae from its shell. "They're cleaning it – and getting fed at the same time."

Orin smiled. Everything was starting to slot into place now. It was all around them in the ocean, nature, creatures, working together, in harmony. Wasn't that how the Eards and people were meant to be? They'd got it so wrong on Ironhold, and on Natura too.

The turtle gazed down at them with soft, curious eyes. Then with a blink it slowly turned and swam away. They stood on the deck and simply watched as it faded into the distance.

It was nearing sunset when they reached the small, unmarked island from their map that they'd been aiming for. They anchored their boat and left Cody to look after it while they swam the short distance to shore. It was a simple island, with only a few clusters of trees, and it didn't appear to have any human inhabitants, but it did have a small freshwater supply where they could refill their bottles. The sun was beginning to set, so after a quick look around, they swam back to the boat to dry off and get ready for the night.

The water was nearly perfectly still, and Orin, Cody and Ferelith lay on the boat deck looking up at the night sky. Stars shone impossibly high and achingly beautiful. The moon, almost full, bathed the sails in a gossamer layer of light. In that moment, they felt almost as it they were floating on air, at one with the universe, without a worry in the world.

A shadow slid across the boat. Orin jolted to sit up. A great being leapt out of the sea beside the boat. A chuff of air and water spurted into the sky and splattered on to the deck.

"It's a wael!" said Ferelith, laughing in the spray. "I've never seen one this close!"

It rolled in the water, and Orin realized that what he'd first thought was the reflection of starlight was actually tiny phosphorescent particles in the water. As the wael softly turned, the bright blue lights danced and spun. Despite its gargantuan size, the creature looked gentle as a snowflake.

Orin sighed happily. If he could stop time, he would stay in this moment for ever.

But they would reach Ironhold soon, and unwelcome thoughts hovered at the back of his mind. Would Commander Forge have assumed he was dead, or would there be guards lying in wait for him? What would he say to his parents? It was all so complicated. He pushed the thoughts away and focused on the stars.

Ferelith looked at him. "You know . . . you never actually told me about the crows and your name, what actually happened."

Cody nodded. "You should tell her the story."

She was right, as she always was. Here, looking up at the dark-blue, velvet sky, it felt right to tell Ferelith the story of his family that Orin always tried to forget. In Grandma's book, she'd written that each star was a story, and for now he tried to pretend that the story he was about to tell was just another Tale of Beyond.

"Once there was an island, a place where dreams, big ideas and new inventions flourished. Every plant was valued and recorded, and every person was an important cog in the wheel. They built, grew and thrived. The engineers had great plans for their island, which they called Ironhold to represent their strength. People were happy, and crops were plentiful. One year a population of crows flew to the island to share in the abundant harvests. But the people had worked hard; the harvests were for them alone. They branded the crows the Cawing Thieves and despaired as crop after crop was eaten. Then a man, Eros Greentip, decided to act. He watched the crows and saw that a minority of the human population had long been encouraging the birds to visit, seeing them as having equal rights to the crops as the human population. Eros Greentip decided that in order to protect what was rightfully the property of the people, they would need to solve the crow problem once and for all."

Orin paused. He hated the next bit.

Ferelith leant in. "Go on."

"Eros Greentip sectioned an area and spread a formula on the crops, concocted by his own hand.

When the crows descended to feed one morning, it seemed like any other day. They ate, then took flight. But then, as though a strange, orchestrated dance had begun, they began dropping from the sky one by one, like black rain. And just like that, Eros, with his poison, rid the island of their crow problem for ever. The birds have never come back." He swallowed, feeling the familiar shame that rushed over him whenever he thought about this story.

"And so it was that Eros Greentip became Eros Crowfall," finished Cody.

"That's my family story," said Orin bitterly. "Saviour of the crops, killer of the innocent. That's my name."

Blowing out a long breath, Ferelith frowned. Above, a shooting star flecked in the night. She put a hand on Orin's arm and gave a gentle smile. "It's a story – and a sad one, for sure. But it's not *your* story. It's the story of Eros, not Orin."

Orin gazed into the night sky. On Ironhold your history defined you. Everything depended on who your family was and what they'd done – where you lived, what you ate, what job you did.

But lying here, under the infinite, dazzling black

sky, he wondered if Ferelith could be right: could he make up his own story? Stories have to start somewhere. Why not start a new one? Why not start with him?

He gave Ferelith a friendly nudge, and, together, the three of them carried on studying the stars.

Sunrise arrived reluctantly and they drew up the anchor and left for the north. There was something pressing and ominous about the new day. Orin thought that all three of them must feel it because none of them exchanged many words all morning, aside from occasional instructions and brief reports.

After midday, there was a sudden drop in the temperature. As far as they knew, there was nothing on the map between themselves and where they estimated Ironhold to be, only the vast ocean. Heading north-westerly, the sea colour changed to a thick dark blue, deep and impenetrable. Orin wondered if they would soon hit the Divide. He hoped they would reach it before nightfall, because facing the sea monster would be bad enough, let alone in darkness.

"I don't think we'll be able to drop anchor tonight," said Cody. "My sonar says it's too deep. So unless things change, we'll have to take turns keeping watch."

Orin nodded. "We're running out of time anyway. But let's keep checking the depth, just in case." He noticed Ferelith shivering.

"How can it be so warm one day, and so freezing the next?" she said between chattering teeth.

"Yet another fault of you humans. Your thin, hairless skin is very sensitive to temperature change." Cody shook her head, then disappeared into the cabin. She returned with a bundle of fabric in her arms. "I found this spare sail in the store and repurposed it." She held out a jacket for each of them.

"That's amazing!" Ferelith put hers on.

"Thanks, Cody." Orin put his on too. It wasn't much, but it was far better than before.

A short distance away to the north, what looked to be several huge fish jumped out of the water. "Look!" Ferelith cried. "Let's get a closer look; it's not far out of our way."

Orin was intrigued too, so he whipped the sail

around and changed direction. The creatures were curious and circled them. He was certain he recognized them from Grandma's book. "Cody, Grandma drew these! Fish-fins or something, aren't they?"

"Dolphins," Cody corrected him. "It's a good job one of us has a photographic memory." She dipped a sonar finger in the water and frowned.

"What is it?"

"The depths are all over the place around here."

"How can that be?"

Numerous dark shapes lurked in the water below, but it was difficult to make them out. Orin strained to see. "What are they? Cody, can you amplify your torchlight and shine it underwater?"

"Give me a moment to reconfigure." She leant over the side and extended her arm, and a light flicked on beneath. "Hold on, let me see if I can make it brighter."

The light intensified, and the sight below took their breath away. It was as though the up-top world had been turned upside down. The broken bones of buildings reached up to them from far below. A whole city under the waves, made up of structures that looked eerily similar to Ironhold.

"What is this place?" asked Ferelith. "What are the unnatural shapes?"

"They're buildings." Orin shivered. Was this what happened if cities failed their Eards? Did they sink to the depths, never to be seen again? It was a stark reminder of why he needed to get back and save his family, and the hundreds of families who were going to be abandoned by the person they had entrusted as their leader. But how—

"You've got that look in your eye again," said Cody.

"No, I haven't," he said defensively.

With a shrug, Cody looked away.

"I never imagined a place could fill me with such sadness," said Ferelith, who was still staring at the gloom below. She looked across at him. "Do you think no one cared enough? That's why it drowned?"

Orin knew how she felt, but he didn't know the answer. "Even if a person cares, is it enough? What can one person do?"

With a tilt of her head, Ferelith gave him a quizzical frown. "What can one person do? Orin, are you actually aware of the things you did back on Natura? You do realize you single-handedly took on the Eärd and somehow won?"

He hadn't thought about it like that.

She shook her head. "You're braver than you realize."

"That's what I keep telling him," said Cody.

Unable to drop anchor, they sailed through the night. Dawn broke with an unwanted frost and another grey-blanketed sky. Their clothes and sail canvas were stiff with ice. They huddled together as much as they could, but nothing could stop their teeth rattling and their fingers burning cold as they repeatedly scraped the sails of ice.

Soon a flurry of white snowflakes tumbled from the sky, to Ferelith's bewilderment. "What is this stuff?"

"Snow. Haven't you ever seen it?"

Shaking her head, she shivered again. "It's beautiful, but I'm too cold to smile."

"If Cody's calculations are correct, we should be at Ironhold by morning."

Two more days before Ironhold and all its people would be abandoned to the sea. To become a sad, forgotten place like the one they'd just seen under the waves. Time was slipping through Orin's fingers.

The snowstorm intensified in the afternoon. For a while they almost came to a standstill, unable to scrape the snow as fast as it fell, and their boat became engulfed by churning, white, freezing seawater. They had no choice but to give in to the greater force and wait it out in the cabin, huddled together. Their faces burned with cold and their jaws and limbs were so frozen they could hardly talk or move. The wind howled and the sea creaked and moaned with ice as it threatened to enclose the boat. Cody did her best to warm them with her internal heating system, but even that was failing. She'd become weak and stiff in her movements.

"Cody, you ... need to go into ... rest mode," Orin stammered.

"I can't ... you'll—"

"Don't ... say it."

"Please, Cody, your power supply ... can't take much more ... too weak... Please. We'll be ... all right." He was angry at the doubt that crept into his voice, but soon Cody's eyes lost their light as she went into sleep mode. She had done it without putting up much of a fight, so he knew she must have been on her lowest reserves.

Ferelith squeezed his arm. "Are you scared?" she whispered.

"Yes," said Orin, his own voice ghostly.

"Me too."

Orin shut his eyes, one arm hooked with Ferelith, the other with Cody, teeth chattering and cold breath mixing as they drifted into frozen sleep.

CHAPTER 20

"Orin, wake up!"

Blinking his eyes open, he was glad to see Ferelith beside him, her cheeks pink with returning warmth, and Cody peering down, holding a steaming drink of something.

"It's just dried nettle tea, I'm afraid. There's nothing much left to eat."

He grasped it gratefully. It was hot, and that was good enough for him.

"What time is it?"

"Morning," Ferelith replied.

"The ice?"

"See for yourself."

Shakily, his muscles feeling like dead wood, he pushed himself to look outside the cabin.

Only disparate patches of ice remained. The grey sky pressed down upon them, but the snowstorm had passed and the wind had dropped. Somehow the morning sun made a veiled appearance far to the east. And to the north, Orin saw a sight that both filled him with relief and chilled him to the bone.

"That's the line. We're nearing the Divide. Be on guard for the mechanical sea monster."

Nobody spoke for a long while. Every creak of wood in the boat sounded amplified.

Orin clutched the oar spear. The line was almost upon them. Beyond that was a thin sea mist. His heart raced. This was it, the place where the mechanical sea monster was programmed to attack oncoming strangers. He scanned the gloom. "Cody, try your radar in the water."

She did, then shrugged and shook her head.

"Where is it?" he breathed.

There was only a boat length until dark water would meet lighter green. They all exchanged glances. It must be nearby.

The line drew closer.

Sweat trickled down Orin's forehead, despite the chill.

And closer.

Then they were over the line, in the domain of Ironhold. Yet still there was no sign of the sea monster.

Orin thought it must be lying in wait, ready to strike suddenly. "Where are you?" he said aloud, his voice thin as the mist.

The boat bobbed and swayed onward.

All at once, a dark shape came into view beyond the fog. An invisible buckle tightened a notch in Orin's belly. But the shape wasn't moving.

His heart leapt as he realized what it was. "We're here. It's Ironhold."

The great spearheads of the towers came into view, majestic and fierce. Orin was elated – they had done it, they were back! – but Ironhold seemed to have fallen into great decline since he'd left. Some buildings looked as though parts had fallen, and there were great cracks in the landscape. Chunks of cliff had fallen in the sea, and a dense menacing sphere of cloud was suspended above the island.

"Wow, that's some island," said Ferelith, leaning

on the edge of the boat, her eyes wide and curious. "Everything is so tall ... and there's nothing green anywhere!"

"It's different here," said Orin.

"Like night is to day; part of the same cycle but opposite," added Cody.

"That was a bit profound for a fixie," Orin teased.

"You can only dream of my kind of brainpower." Cody winked.

Despite his joy at almost being home, panic rose in Orin's throat the closer they got to Ironhold. "We should stay back a little, in case they're watching." He was fairly certain that Commander Forge must think him dead by now, but he didn't want to take any chances.

They were thankful of the patches of sea mist concealing them as they neared the eastern side of the island. To the distant eye, they would hopefully look like just another fishing boat.

"We'll have less distance to travel on the island if we land on the other side, near West Tip. If we can sneak on to the beach there, we'll be able to get up to my family."

"And then?" asked Cody.

He knew what she was saying. The problem was bigger than just saving Orin's family. The whole of Ironhold was on the brink of destruction. But if he didn't save them all, then who would? Besides, he wasn't alone. He had Cody and Ferelith by his side. He just wished he had a plan.

As they circled Ironhold to the north, Orin saw something through the fog. A canopy had been erected on the shore, and along from it, inert at the jetty, was the mechanical sea monster. Its enormous orange, metallic body was laid out and rested in one long cylinder, its huge serpent head with its great jagged teeth looking out to sea, although it looked to be inactive, as its eye receptors were unlit and dull.

"That's what attacked you?" Ferelith said as she spotted it, her voice filled with horror.

"Keep down," Cody urged. "There are engineers there."

Orin and Ferelith ducked.

"What can you see?"

"It looks like they're loading supplies."

"The Core engineers must be planning on leaving in the sea monster! That's how they're going to get to their new island."

The beginnings of an idea sparked in Orin's head.

Silently, they sailed on into the mist, tracking the dark silhouette of the island until they found the west beach. They waded into the water to pull the boat up the small shore, then attached the boat by rope to a boulder.

Orin couldn't believe his feet were finally back on Ironhold, but it didn't feel like home; it felt like danger. He looked around to make sure there was no one about. There wasn't – and the reason why soon became clear. The cliff to the south of the beach had part-crumbled into the sea, and there were big splits in some of the boulders. The beach was unusable for fishing; it was too dangerous.

Ferelith was looking up at the buildings of West Tip, her mouth wide in astonishment. "How do they all stay standing?"

"It can feel a bit scary at times, especially in a storm, but you get used to it." After being in Natura, everything in Ironhold seemed so angular to Orin. The buildings were familiar, but it was as though he'd grown apart from the place too, and a strange emptiness seemed to be growing within him. It was probably the worry of what lay ahead, he realized.

They climbed the rock steps towards West Tip. The buildings creaked and moaned in the wind as if they were complaining against the grip of the ominous surrounding clouds.

"Here, this way. My house isn't far." Nervous excitement and fear tangled in Orin's stomach. What would his parents say when he opened the door? He didn't want to shock or upset them, but he couldn't think of any way of returning without any element of surprise. The light was on in the kitchen window.

Before he grasped the handle, he paused. So much had happened since he'd last been here. Orin had imagined this moment since he'd watched the outline of Ironhold fade into the distance only nine days previously. If he was going to save Ironhold, it would start with his family.

His dad was the first person to see him when he opened the door. His copper hair seemed to be larger and wilder than ever. There was a moment when time stood still, before he dropped the mug of tea he was holding.

"Orin? It can't be." He looked at him as though he was a ghost for a moment. "Estri! Come quickly!"

A great surge of warmth filled Orin. There were so many times he'd thought this moment would never happen.

Grandpa looked up from the fireplace. He jumped out of his chair as though he was suddenly twenty years younger and grabbed Orin into a bone-crushing hug. "But what . . . how . . . where?"

"It's a long story, Grandpa." The familiar smoky smell of Grandpa's shirt tugged at Orin's heart.

Mum rushed in and let out a yelp of disbelief, then joined them in the family embrace, and they all let the tears of relief flow. Seeing his family again was like the sun breaking through clouds after a storm. He breathed in their familiar scent, warm fires and the oils of the fixie factory.

"I can't believe you're here! Commander Forge said there'd been a fishing accident," said Estri. "She came to tell us herself. She said you'd likely got caught on the tide and accidentally gone beyond the Divide, and then the mechanical sea monster. . ."

"There's a lot to tell you, Mum." His family all looked so tired and drawn, as though they had barely slept this past week.

Ferelith stood quietly in the doorway.

"Who's this?" asked Estri, noticing her.

"This is Ferelith. A friend."

"From West Tip? I don't recognize her," said Grandpa.

"No, Grandpa, not from West Tip. She's from a long way away."

"Not East Ironhold, surely?"

"No, Grandpa," Orin said, with a smile. "She's from an island, like from the stories in Grandma's book. I got chased out to sea – there was a storm and I crashed on her island. But that doesn't matter now. The Eard of Ironhold is in trouble. Commander Forge has been taking its life-light." His words tumbled out. He knew he wasn't telling it quite right. The words sounded strange and unbelievable, even to his own ears, but he had to make his parents understand. "They're going to drain it one last time and then Ironhold will crumble into the sea..." He tailed off. His family were looking at him in confusion,

"Whatever do you mean?" asked Dad.

"I overheard things at the Engineerium, and Commander Forge caught me and chased me out to sea, then a storm came and I ended up on an island.

Ferelith saved my life, and so did Cody."

"Your fixie?" said Grandpa.

Orin sighed. His parents were exchanging confused glances. This was going to be harder than he'd thought. How would he make them believe the seemingly unbelievable?

Estri ushered Ferelith in. "Sit by the fire. You poor things are freezing."

Orin let his parents take over, and tiredness flooded through him. Outside, the streets might be different from how he remembered them, but inside his home smelt of the same warm, woody aroma of the fire, the same cups and saucers were stacked on the dresser, he saw the same knitted rainbow mats and armchairs, and most importantly, his parents and Grandpa were the same. He wondered what Ferelith made of it. He glanced at her and she flashed a warm smile, although her eyes told him she was nervous.

"I think we need to all have a long chat," said Dad. "You said a lot of words then and not many of them made sense, if I'm honest."

"What did you mean about the Eard being in trouble? Commander Forge protects it." Mum frowned. "Did you hit your head?"

It had never been more wonderful to hear Mum's ever-concerned tone.

Grandpa leant in, his eyes bright with curiosity, moustache twiddled into two large curls. "And what's this life-light you mentioned?"

By the time Orin had finished telling the family the story for a second time, the sleepy fire had nearly gone out. Nobody spoke for a long while.

Mum stood up to stoke the fire. The embers awakened with an orange glow and warmed the room. "It's a lot to take in, Orin."

"It really *is* all true," said Ferelith.

After exchanging another furtive glance with Mum, Dad said, "There have been whispered worries about Commander Forge – neglecting repairs, structural concerns about her new buildings. But that doesn't mean she's going to abandon Ironhold. Are you absolutely certain of what you saw?"

"Absolutely. Dad, all the cracks and collapses are nothing to do with freak storms, it's all connected. It's because of what she's doing to the Eard. She's neglecting the repairs because she's going to leave it all behind." He looked each one of his family in the eye in turn, then said firmly, "You *have* to believe me. There's no time left."

Grandpa tapped his fingers on the arm of the chair thoughtfully. "Grandma always said Forge was wrong for bringing in the mechanical sea monster, that protecting Ironhold was a load of nonsense. Perhaps Commander Forge was ensuring she kept the power to herself. Keeping the people fearful of outsiders is a good way to ensure the focus is on others as the problem, and so stop them looking too closely at what goes on inside. So, yes, Orin. What you say might seem unbelievable, but it doesn't mean it's not the truth." He patted him on the knee.

"But what about the mark on her hand? That proves she's been chosen to look after the Eard – she would never betray that sacred bond," said Mum.

"I think it might be . . . fake." It was all starting to make sense now, the memories slotting into place. "I saw one of the medi-bots patching it up, although I didn't realize it at the time. But when I went to Natura, I learned that *anyone* can communicate with an Eard. Commander Forge wants us to believe she's the only one who can do it, so she can use its power."

Ferelith stood up. "You should have seen your son when everyone else was too afraid to stand up to our Eard."

His parents exchanged another look, and this time they gave a nod to each other; Orin knew they believed him.

"OK, Orin. What's next?" asked Mum.

"Yes, what *are* we going to do?" asked Ferelith.

Orin took a deep breath. "At first, I thought we could get away on boats and sail to an island far away, but there are hundreds of people here and they'll never believe me over Commander Forge." He shook his head. "Besides. This is our home. Who knows what it could become if we actually looked after our Eard?" He thought of Natura and the wonderful creatures and plants that thrived there. He thought of the harmony and balance he'd seen between the creatures they'd met at sea. That was what it should be like; that was what they were fighting for.

"So, what's your plan?" said Grandpa.

Orin glanced at Cody, who had been sitting a short distance from the fire warming her circuits, pretending she was like any other fixie now she was back in the Crowfall home.

"The Core are loading up the mechanical sea monster. We're going to take pictures as evidence tonight when no one's around, and then we're going to try and reprogramme the sea monster with new instructions and send it out to sea. We'll upload the picture evidence to the morning transmission. If the people see what Commander Forge is doing, and if the Core haven't got a way to escape, they'll *have* to stop."

"Orin, what you've been through, what you've done these past weeks is incredible. But you're no engineer," said Dad. "How will you reprogramme a machine as sophisticated as that?"

Orin looked at Cody. "How do you fancy a bit of reprogramming?"

She smiled. "I thought you'd never ask."

CHAPTER 21

"Ah, happy to speak in front of us now, are you?" asked Grandpa, looking over at Cody.

"Wait. You knew? All along?" said Orin, exchanging a puzzled glance with Cody, who shrugged.

"Of course!" said Dad. "But you were so keen on keeping it secret. We trusted you knew what you were doing and left you to it."

"We knew you'd tell us more when you were ready." Mum smiled. She pulled Orin into another hug, her brown curls enveloping him. "I can't believe you're really here."

"Right, let's make you two a good meal," said

Grandpa. "You look skinny as beans, and there's no sense saving any food stores if things are going the way you say. I'll cook you up a feast."

After a breakfast of everything Grandpa could find to cook, they went over their plans together. They had to wait for it to get dark and couldn't risk going outside the house and being seen yet, so they made the best use of the time they could by going over their plans and drawing maps. In the afternoon, Grandpa brought some spare blankets into Orin's room, watered the juniper sapling and other plants, which he'd looked after diligently since Orin had left, then insisted they try to get some rest before the evening.

Despite the exhausting journey across the sea, Orin found it hard to nap. What would happen if they failed? Cody was in the living space, accessing the main communication system, Ironcom, which brought transmission news from the Engineerium. She thought she should be able to hack into some of the engineers' files and find the blueprints for the mechanical sea monster. At the same time, Cody and Grandpa were having a happy conversation about recipes and how Cody could adapt her screwdriver attachment as a whisk.

"Are you awake?" Orin whispered.

After a pause, Ferelith said, "I am now."

"What are you thinking about?"

"That we should get some sleep."

"What if everything goes wrong?"

Ferelith propped herself up on her elbow. "Are you having doubts? You sounded very certain, speaking to your parents."

"I know, I had to be, or they'd think we couldn't do it."

She sighed. "Go to sleep, Orin, and wake up more positive."

Quiet as shadows, Orin, Ferelith and Cody crept into the midnight streets of West Tip. They decided to take a boat and approach from the water, as there would be less chance of being seen. They chose a tiny rowing boat used for collecting clams from the areas unreachable by foot; it was smaller than their sailboat and less likely to be seen. Their oars sliced through the water, the sound masked by the perpetual low growl of the dark cloud above the city. Patches of sea mist dampened their clothes, although Orin was too full of adrenaline to feel the cold. The waves were neither still nor angry, but after four days at sea he found he could read their push and pull, and his arms felt strong. On the other side of the boat, Ferelith mirrored his movements. Mum and Dad had tried to insist that one of them come along too, and in the end, it had been Cody who had explained the logic of keeping their numbers low by reeling off statistics and probabilities of being seen depending on different scenarios. Baffled by her numbers, they agreed it was safer for them to stay at home. And they couldn't argue that Orin and Ferelith had proved themselves capable on their own.

As they neared, Orin indicated to pause the rowing. The sea monster's eye lights were off, but a lamp was lit at the very end of the jetty, revealing the long, segmented cylindrical outline of the sea monster. A single guard stood beneath the light.

"What is that thing?" breathed Ferelith.

"One of Commander Forge's robot guards." The sight of it made Orin's hands tighten on the oars, but he tried not to show his tension in his voice. "Don't worry. It's facing the street. If we drift to the furthest end of the jetty and tie off on the other side, we'll be out of sight."

Cody dimmed her eyes to their lowest setting. "The blueprints detailed several hatches. The monster has been put into rest mode, and the safest thing will be to take the front hatch nearest its head. But the storage sectors are further down, and that's where we need to get the evidence."

Orin understood what she was saying. "We'll need to take the pictures before reprogramming, so we go for the middle hatch."

When they were close enough, Orin held the boat steady while Ferelith climbed on to the jetty. Cody threw her the rope, and she tied the boat to the jetty hooks at the front and back. Before Orin and Cody left the boat, Orin took something from his pocket and handed it to Cody. "Socks."

"You shouldn't have. It's not even my birthday," she said.

"They're to dampen your footsteps, silly. Your feet will echo against metal."

Cody nodded, reluctantly impressed. "That's actually not bad thinking for a human brain."

She slipped them on, and he lifted her over

the side to Ferelith and climbed out himself. The mechanical sea monster was huge beside them. Scare bumps prickled his arms; there was something eerie about the motionless metal giant, as though it was waiting. Ferelith pulled his arm and gestured for him to follow Cody, who was heading for a metal panel with a hatch. She pressed what looked to be a rivet, and a palm-sized flap opened in the side, something like the entry doors in the Engineerium.

Cody proceeded to press a combination of buttons, and then a loud hiss of air sounded, making them all recoil. The panel moved several inches towards them, then slid up to reveal an opening. They glanced down the jetty in case the guard had heard.

Orin's muscles were poised for action. Should they run back for the boat, or jump inside and seal the door behind them? Thankfully the guard didn't seem to have noticed, and as Orin turned to tell the others it was all right, he saw Ferelith was already stepping inside. Despite the nerves tingling his belly, he couldn't help smiling. Ferelith was gutsy, a born adventurer. The thought of Thao and the Eard trying to contain her was laughable now he knew her. It would only have been a matter of time before she found a way off the island.

Cody lit her finger torch. "The monster's sensors are in sleep mode, so it won't feel or hear us." She shone the light towards the back end.

"Look at all this stuff!" whispered Ferelith. The central cavity was filled with chests and crates of dried food, cans, tools, books, and various other materials.

"They sure mean business," said Cody, her eyes flashing with a pulse of light as she committed an image to her memory bank.

"Take lots of pictures. We'll need plenty to convince the people that Commander Forge and the Core mean to abandon them and never return."

They huddled around, opening various crates while Cody took the pictures. Orin noticed one of the chests had a tiny sliver of light at the edge of the lid. "Cody, open this one. I think I know what's inside," he said urgently.

Her screwdriver finger whirred and they removed the lid. Vials of life-light shone, their silvery glow reflecting off their noses and chins as the three peered inside.

"That's what they extracted from the Eard?" said Ferelith with a shiver.

For a moment, Orin wondered what it would feel like to drink one, to have the serene strength of Commander Forge and know that you could live for ever. Would you become so absorbed in the power that you wouldn't care about the consequences? He shuddered. He would never understand how she could justify doing something so terrible to another living creature. For a moment he thought about tipping the life-light into the sea so that no one could use it, but it was part of the Eard and it didn't seem right.

"Make sure we have lots of pictures of these," he said.

When they were satisfied, they made their way towards the head cavity of the monster. "Time for the tricky bit," said Cody.

"Do we need to reprogramme it? Maybe the pictures will be enough?" said Ferelith.

Orin shook his head. "What if they try for a quick escape even if they don't manage to drain the life-light? We need to get this monster far away so they don't stand a chance."

Towards the front they found the main controls,

a large, complicated mix of wires and components situated behind the head.

"It's like tangled water-weed." Ferelith frowned.

"Is there anything we can do to help?" Orin asked Cody, feeling suddenly useless. So much of his plan rested on her abilities.

"Just watch out for that guard. I need to reconfigure the central processing signal and send a looping message to the motion sensors and. . ." She paused. "You don't know what I'm talking about, do you?"

Orin shook his head. "Not a clue, buddy. But I do trust you."

"Sometimes I wonder how you managed to connect my power source in the first place."

"With a big manual and a lot of time. That's why I prefer plants – much simpler. How long will it take?"

"Under a centiday." Cody began extending wires and sensors from her own fingers and connecting them with the sea monster's control panel.

With a nudge to his ribs, Ferelith passed him something. "I found this in one of the crates. It smells really good."

"Chocolate!" he spluttered. "That's worth a year's credits at least! The cocoa bean tree is one of the most precious in the growing towers. No one is even allowed in there, apart from the lead cultivator."

Ferelith stuffed a large chunk into her mouth.

"Wait, you can't just—"

"Oh my, it's delicious," she muttered through a full mouth.

Orin looked at the velvety, brown chunk in his hand. The scent made his mouth water, but he hesitated. People from West Tip didn't get to eat things like chocolate.

Ferelith swallowed. "What are you waiting for?"

She was right. He took a bite. An explosion of sweet richness erupted in his mouth. "No wonder they keep it to themselves! Did you take any more?"

"I filled my pockets," she sniggered.

Cody glanced over. "If you two have quite finished, I'm getting to the final part, but it's up there and I can't reach without my wings."

"Oh, sorry," said Orin, lifting her on to his shoulders.

"Right, move over a little. I need to get to this last panel, where the wires meet the main power supply." She lifted a flap and they both paused, amazed. Inside, something glowed. A sphere sparkled with glittery sparks of light.

Orin recognized it instantly. "It's one of the pods from the Eard. It's the same as I used to power you."

"Oh, that's an Eard seed. I've seen them on the Eard of Natura," said Ferelith. "They're pretty rare; Thao said you get one seed a year, if you're lucky."

"It's pretty amazing to think that one of these seeds is part of me, that it's a part of why I think like I do." She shook her head. "But logic tells me we'll have lots of time to get philosophical about that after we've completed the mission." She locked a sensor onto one of the wires. "Right, I'm reconfiguring the signal and—"

Metal groaned.

"What was that?"

They looked at one another, their eyes wide and alert.

Cody gave a nervous laugh. "It was nothing, I'm sure. Be quiet, I need to concentrate."

Two large lights flickered in the head cavity.

"That's part of the reconfiguring, right, Cody?"

"It shouldn't be, I'm not finish—"

The body of the mechanical sea monster shuddered, vibrating through their feet into their legs and bodies. The flickering lights illuminated to full brightness. They were the two eyes of the mechanical sea monster set within its great head.

The Sentinel was awake.

CHAPTER 22

The creak of metal was deafening. The sea monster jerked, sending them bouncing up in the cavity.

With Cody still on Orin's shoulders, they were thrust violently towards the ceiling. A great *clang* sounded as Cody hit the metal above, her body protecting Orin from a more powerful impact. They landed back on the floor with a thud.

"Are you all right?" Orin grasped Cody's dented body.

She nodded. "Yes, but something tells me it knows we're in here."

Ferelith was rubbing her ankle. "What just happened?"

"Maybe a glitch with the reprogramming. Did

you manage to finish?"

Cody's eyes flickered. "Well, almost. I just need—"

There was another almighty *bang* and they were thrown to the side. Orin's shoulder smashed painfully into metal. Before they could recover, the sea monster thrust in the opposite direction, sending them tumbling again.

"I think we're definitely finished," said Cody. "We need to get out of here, now!"

"There's a hatch," shouted Ferelith.

Another jolt propelled them upwards, and from outside came the ping of rope and ripping of wood.

Orin recovered first. "Come on!" He lifted Cody up to a panel to release the hatch. She swiftly tapped buttons and it opened with a loud *hiss*. The moonlit storm cloud above the island came into view. "Quick, we need to get out, and back to the boat."

But with heart-sinking realization, Orin saw that the sea monster had broken free from the jetty, which was now a metre or so away. "Hold on to my shoulders, Cody: we'll have to jump. After three. One, two..." They perched on the edge of the opening, ready to leap, but with a roar, the sea monster ripped its tail end free and they were lifted into the air.

Orin's heart jumped to his throat, but he and Ferelith somehow managed to cling to the door rim, Cody's hands clutched tightly around his neck.

With a whip of its tail, the sea monster bore down on the jetty, smashing through it – and their small rowing boat – in an explosion of wood. The monster began moving away from the island at great speed.

"Jump!" Orin yelled to Ferelith, and they propelled themselves away from the sea monster and into the biting cold water.

The air was snatched from Orin's lungs. He rolled and churned beneath the water, desperately trying to distinguish up from down. A sickening jolt hit him as metal flashed, and he realized the tail of the sea monster was heading towards him. Cody was still clinging to his neck. As they rose upwards, the tail smashed, hitting her and missing him. He broke the surface and gulped for air.

"Cody! Ferelith!" he called.

Cody was gone, and he couldn't see Ferelith anywhere. All around was black as basalt. The sea monster was moving further into the distance now, perhaps turning for an attack. They had to get back to shore. Forcing himself beneath the waves, he searched for reflected light and movement, for any sign of his friends, but soon his lungs burned for breath and he had to surface again.

Panic coursed through him. Where were they?

Then, not far away, Ferelith burst from beneath the waves. To his relief she was clutching Cody.

"Get to the shore!" he called. He darted a glance behind, but there was no longer any sign of the sea monster, so he kicked and followed Ferelith's bobbing head in the direction of the shore. "Are you all right?" he gasped, between heaves of breath.

"Just," replied Ferelith.

"Me too!" shouted Cody.

"Let's head to the west, away from the jetty." The guards would be on alert now. Hopefully they would be too busy with the sea monster breaking away to worry about them.

It was biting cold and his muscles felt like lead, every stroke like swimming through tar, but Orin felt a surge of hope. Cody had the images from inside the sea monster as evidence of what Commander Forge was planning, and they had removed Forge's means of escaping the island. Maybe it would delay the last drain of the Eard's life-light long enough for the other engineers to rebel.

Aiming for the small west jetty, Orin thought they'd be able to take the edge path up towards West Tip. As they neared the shore, the waves pounded relentlessly, and by the time Orin's hands grasped the wood of the small jetty, it was all he could do to cling on and catch his breath. He'd kept Cody and Ferelith in sight the whole way ahead of him, and they'd come ashore at the end of the jetty on the beach. Ferelith cradled Cody and sat panting behind a large rock. Using his last strength, Orin pulled himself up and crawled along the jetty in their direction and was nearly there when, to his dismay, footsteps sounded close by, too light for guards' feet. He glanced across to Ferelith and Cody, a knot tightening in his stomach.

"Get the evidence on the network," he whispered.

Then a voice, unnervingly quiet in the night, spoke his name. "Orin Crowfall. Just where I left you."

Orin looked up and with a horrifying lurch, found himself staring up into the steel-blue eyes of Commander Forge.

*

A guard wasn't far behind Commander Forge, and he quickly tied Orin's hands behind his back. At least they hadn't seen Ferelith and Cody behind the rock, so perhaps, even though fear froze his veins, his capture would be a good enough distraction to allow Ferelith and Cody to do what was needed.

"Well, well. Somehow you survived." Commander Forge pulled down the hood of her white cloak. The metal-bladed layers of her epaulettes and the spliced V symbol of Ironhold pinning her cape gleamed with the light from the jetty. Her eyes continued to bore into him, her skin porcelain in the night, hair bright as blood. "Tell me, how could one weak boy from West Tip possibly survive a great storm on the ocean and the Sentinel?"

Her voice was curious, almost admiring.

He found he couldn't reply. His throat felt gripped by invisible hands.

"Did you really think you could stop me by reprogramming the Sentinel? Although I must admit, these skills are far beyond what I'd expect from a West Tip boy. I underestimated you."

Good, he thought. She hadn't realized about Cody.

She narrowed her eyes. "Perhaps you had help. The fixie that was with you when you left the island . . . it didn't behave like an ordinary fixie." She looked to the guard. "Search the beach."

"Just you wait." His voice was raspy. "You'll see what she can do. She's still inside the sea monster."

Forge narrowed her eyes, and for a moment Orin felt as though she was reading his very soul, and he tried to imagine a wall around the lie.

"Guard, forget the beach. Send a message to the Core to meet at the Engineerium. Tell them the time has come." She sighed. "I will have to personally reprogramme the Sentinel to stop your little friend and have it return here, of course, and you –" she looked to Orin – "are coming with me."

The guard dragged Orin through to the doors of room 505.

Commander Forge sat down at the great table.

"Fetch me a drink, server," she ordered Orin.

The guard relaxed its grip, and Orin shook out his hands, barely able to feel them. Still dripping from the sea and shivering, he went to the cabinet, fetched a cup and filled it with juice from the cold cabinet.

Commander Forge flipped open a compartment in the table, and a hologram appeared which detailed hundreds of numbers and symbols. She began moving her fingers within them, like a dance.

He stood shivering at the edge of the room, the guard by the door watching his every move.

Outside, the new day bled on to the horizon of the eastern sea, while above black clouds circled. Orin's parents would have expected him back by now and would be worried. He prayed that somewhere Cody was uploading the images to the Ironhold morning transmission. After a milliday tapping at the numbers and manipulating calculations, Commander Forge leant back. "There, it will return. Your attempt was a mere inconvenience." Her head angled with a quizzical tilt as she observed Orin once more. "You really thought you could stop us? That a nothing boy could stop the natural, evolutionary next step for humankind?"

Anger rushed through his veins. This was his chance to tell her what he thought of her. "You know that taking the Eard's life-light is destroying Ironhold. But what about the people, and the Eard itself? Don't you care?"

Commander Forge smiled sweetly. "All this, even the Eard, is fleeting, but we, the Core, have the possibility of for ever. I don't suppose you can imagine such power."

"I can imagine the damage it causes," he said scathingly.

"For a while. But some things must be sacrificed for a new, purer way."

He thought of the skeleton city beneath the sea. All the animals and plant life that had been committed to a ghostly life beneath the waves. Was that what was to become of Ironhold. "Sacrificed?"

She gave a nod. "A necessary sacrifice, because for those who matter, the future is secured."

He couldn't believe what he was hearing. She really thought this was the next step for human evolution.

"Come on. It's time for the final spectacle. You can have a front row seat."

CHAPTER 23

Orin had never been in Commander Forge's private Engineerium lift before. It was the only lift that wasn't glass and ran through the centre of the building. The robot guard marched him inside. The walls were smooth and white, and you could barely see where they met the ceiling and floor. There were no buttons, just a small microphone imbedded in one wall.

"To the heart," Forge said.

The lift lurched down.

When they stepped out, the other nine members of the Core were waiting, all dressed in their immaculate red cloaks, Ironhold pins polished. Orin had seen this area of the Eard from above when he'd seen Forge take its life-light, before he'd realized she was harming it in the most terrible of ways. The heart of the Eard was an underground cavern, earthy and damp, with roots and branches trailing the walls, floor and ceiling. But now they were mostly shrivelled and dead, with patches of mould growing in places. The rot he'd wanted to treat with his potion before had completely taken over. It was so far from the thriving creature the Eard of Natura was.

Instinctively, he reached for a root in the wall beside him and tried to tell it he was sorry – for how it had been treated all these years, for what was about to happen. The guard shoved him forward before his hand could make contact.

"Is everything all right?" Silver Blecher asked nervously.

The commander nodded calmly. "Of course. And what better way to start the day than with life-light?"

Ten more guards appeared, each holding an iron-and-glass stabbing spear like the one he'd seen Commander Forge with the last time he was here. The spears all had the same great bulbous containers attached to the ends, ready to collect the Eard's life-light. Orin's stomach twisted. He looked up at the small amount of daylight coming from the conservatory roof that enclosed the Eard above. Crossing his fingers, he willed that any moment now someone would arrive, to help. They would have seen the pictures, they would come. *Someone* would stop this.

A scream that would turn water to stone echoed around the chamber. Commander Forge had thrust her spear into the Eard. The others followed, and Orin grasped his ears to block out the awfulness of the sound.

Everything around him tensed. Luminous silver liquid began flowing into the spears from the roots, the white sparks of light leaving behind angry purple and black veins. Huge patches of the Eard were dying.

"Stop it!" Orin yelled. "You're killing it!"

"Quiet, foolish boy," said Commander Forge, her eyes wild with power.

The ground rumbled, but still Forge continued. Orin tried to break free from the guard, but the robot's grip was impossibly strong. He yelled again as a great crack appeared above and fragments of the ceiling rained down.

"Please!" he cried.

Somehow he pulled an arm free and he reached out, touching a root. A great chasm opened inside of him, filled with the Eard's pain and sadness. It made every sinew strain, as though he was falling from a great height and all he could feel was deep, wrenching sorrow. Once more he heard a voice somewhere inside of him as light as starlight and deep as the earth, yet different to the Eard of Natura's voice.

Too much suffering. Too weak.

The Eard of Ironhold was so tired, its voice echoed as though from a distant land. "Hold on," he breathed. "Commander Forge, you have to stop!" He tried again, but the silver liquid was already cascading into the vessels. Commander Forge was taking every last drop.

Then a faint murmur, shadowed and distant. *Everything will be all right.*

The gloom and pain and the blackness inside widened, filling his chest, his torso, his limbs until it was everywhere, and everything went dark.

Orin woke in a room made of glass. The ceiling came to a point. Where was he? Where were the

Core? There was only one place with a great glass point in Ironhold, he realized. He was still in the Engineerium, at the very top floor. The sky outside was dark as night, thick with rolling angry clouds. How long had he been unconscious?

All around were creaks and groans. A flash of lightning made him jolt, and simultaneous thunder boomed. He scurried to the only door, made of metal and thick glass. His hands were tied together in front, so he turned the doorknob and pulled, but of course it was locked tight, the key on the other side.

The Core had drained the Eard. All his plans had come to nothing.

Yet ... somehow, he could feel it was still alive down there. But barely. Was there still a chance to save it?

Outside, the crashing sounds continued. What was going on? He pushed himself to standing and staggered to the glass. A scene of devastation faced him: cracking towers, falling debris, people far below running, panicked. Whole towers had fallen in the east! He couldn't breathe. Commander Forge had done exactly what she'd said – and she'd sent Ironhold into a final spiral of destruction.

His family and friends were out there, somewhere! He had to find them. He ran to the door again and banged. There was no one in the corridor beyond. It looked like everyone had abandoned the building, even the guards. Another bolt of lightning flashed, hitting the lightning rod atop the Engineerium roof. The crack was deafening, and Orin fell to the ground as the whole tower shook. The window glass began splintering like creeping veins.

With all certainty, Orin knew the tower would fall. He had to get out, and fast.

Pounding the door, he screamed for help. "Please!" he begged.

How had it come to this? Closing his eyes, he wished for time to go backwards, to the days when things seemed simple and he didn't feel the weight of the whole world on his shoulders. He thought of climbing the cliffs with Cody, how they would laugh at the silliest things, hugs with his parents and his grandpa, the moments of happiness he'd felt sailing the oceans with Ferelith.

Then he opened his eyes and saw a figure run out of the stairwell outside the door. She was filthy with dust, her clothes were torn in places, her hair was bedraggled, but her eyes were bright with emerald fire. Her mouth opened, and although he couldn't hear through the glass, he knew she had called his name.

"Ferelith!"

In moments, she'd unlocked the door and grabbed him into an embrace. "Orin!"

Cody clattered along behind her. Her body was badly crumpled and one antenna hung loose.

"You lost the socks," he half-cried, half-laughed with relief.

"They didn't suit me." Cody smiled.

Ferelith grabbed his shoulders. "You're all right. What happened?"

"Commander Forge... The Core... They drained every last drop of the life-light. We failed." He tried to contain the tears, but it was making his eyes ache to hold them in. "I'm sorry I let you all down. If she hadn't caught me on the beach..."

"Let us down? How is this your fault? No one could have tried harder, Orin. Do you hear me?" Ferelith grasped his face until he nodded. "Anyway, we didn't completely fail."

Cody nodded. "We managed to get the images

into the morning transmission. The other engineers know what the Core was up to. But they didn't reach the Engineerium in time to stop Commander Forge."

He shook his head. "It's not much consolation. The Core must be long gone by now."

Ferelith shook her head. A satisfied smile tinging the edges. "Cody knew about Commander Forge's reprogramming of the sea monster. She let Forge do it, then when she'd finished, Cody sent it away again! It stayed away, so Forge must have been too busy draining the life-light to notice!"

Cody gave a wink. "Humans: mostly only able to focus on one thing at a time."

Pride filled Orin's chest and he raised a hand to high-five Cody. "You never let me down."

Then the room started vibrating again.

"Everything is falling apart. We have to go," said Ferelith. Hurriedly, she untied Orin's hands and they ran down the stairs. "This magic box machine is still working. Thankfully, Cody knows how to run it."

"You mean the lift? It's not actually magic." He raised his eyebrows.

"Orin, this is hardly the time to get technical!"

He smiled. He felt another mad surge of hope.

Against the odds, they were together. They would do whatever it took to save Ironhold. They hurried inside and Ferelith jabbed the button for the ground. With a lurch, they began descending.

"How did you find me?"

"We figured Forge would have brought you here. After she took you, we went back to West Tip, and Cody used your home transmitter to get the images out. But then the clouds grew angry and orange, and buildings started cracking everywhere. . . It was terrifying. The ground rumbled and at first all we could do was cling on."

He was so grateful to them. "What about my family? Is West Tip all right?"

Ferelith shook her head sadly. "I have to be honest; I don't know. When we left, it was crumbling to dust."

Cody nodded. "We told your parents and grandpa to get on a boat, but they had an idea to programme the fixies to make more boats quickly, so your mum was working with a group of engineers on that. If we can't stabilize the island, at least we can get everyone safely in a boat."

Pride swelled in Orin's chest at his family's

courage. The lift opened at the ground floor and they ran outside, where hundreds of people had congregated around the Engineerium: green cloaks, brown, grey.

"What are they still doing here? Why aren't they heading for the boats?"

"Most are, but some are still under the illusion that the transmissions must be fake, that the Core is on their side."

An ear-splitting fracture sounded close by. Above, a crack spread like swiftly freezing ice on a pane of glass, fissures sprawling. "These buildings aren't going to last long!" Orin realized in horror. "We need to head for the fixie factory on the north-west side of the island and find my family."

Between crashes of thunder, there were shouts and cries of confusion. People were running in all directions.

"What do we do?"

"The Engineers will save us!"

"There aren't enough boats, they can't make them fast enough!"

Orin, Ferelith and Cody pushed on through the panicked crowds, past cracking buildings towards the north east of the island. At one point, Orin stepped on a battered, fallen placard reading *Industry Brings Prosperity*.

"Ironic," said Cody as a lightning rod crashed to the ground a short distance away.

"Orin!" someone shouted.

Dad pushed through the throng. "Thank goodness you're all right! We put Grandpa and his friends on a boat in the south."

"What about Mum?"

"She's still helping with the boats, but the way back just crumbled completely." He looked panicked, close to tears, his copper hair wilder than ever. "We need to get to a boat. Some people are heading north, near the fixie factory, as there are a few boats left there, and Mum instructed a group of fixies to fly boats to the people gathering on the south-west coast because the land seems more stable there, at least for now."

People barged into them in panic and Dad almost fell. Orin grabbed his arm and called to Cody. "Cody, they don't know what to do. The Core have abandoned them, and the comms must be down. Can you programme your voice to full volume? The loudest it can go?"

She nodded.

"Tell them their best chance is to all head to the south-west beach."

Cody nodded, then her voice boomed through the streets. "This is a public announcement. There are boats still on the south-west beach. Citizens should head there swiftly and in orderly fashion! I repeat, the south-west beach."

The people calmed and changed direction.

"Good job, Cody."

In the distant east, more great towers began disappearing, as though the ground beneath had vanished suddenly. The cultivation towers imploded, sending lethal shards of glass shooting across the sky. Screams rang through the air like wind. Dad grabbed Orin's hand. "It's time to leave."

He nodded. "Get to the south-west."

"And you too!"

Orin paused. The way he saw it, there were two possible options: abandon the dying Eard and head for the boats, or, if there was a sliver of life left, stay and try to save Ironhold. And as much as Orin wanted to run to a boat right now, instinct and recent experience told him that there was hope even when things seemed darkest. Perhaps it *was* possible to still help the Eard. But to do that, he needed to turn back.

"We'll follow, but there's something I need to do first." He looked to Ferelith, who seemed to understand – or simply accept – he knew what he was doing, and gave a nod.

If the cultivation towers had gone, it might not be long before the remaining towers of the Engineerium fell too.

When Dad opened his mouth to protest, Orin jumped in. "Dad, we've survived a lot this past week, we'll be all right."

Dad hugged him. "Please be careful. I can't lose you twice."

Orin nodded. "I promise."

With a resigned smile, Dad left.

"What bonkers plan are you conjuring now?" asked Cody.

CHAPTER 24

Orin, Ferelith and Cody sprinted their way back to the Engineerium, dodging past falling bricks, leaping over cracking pavements, and skirting past a sinkhole where there had once been an under-rail. They came upon a group of people not far from the Engineerium who were scared and didn't know what to do, as the way south-west was now blocked, so Orin, Ferelith and Cody helped them around several fallen buildings to find the path north that was luckily still intact. Cody took a nasty blow from a falling steel joist, but insisted she was all right, just dented. Nevertheless, Orin made her cling to his neck for the rest of the journey. On the way, they pulled a small boy trapped by wreckage, and Ferelith hoisted him on to her shoulders, and they all rushed on to the last rocky area of high land in the north, which had once been the recycling plant. Debris churned perilously in the waves, and rocks jutted like giant teeth from the water. In the distance, dozens of boats battled the angry waves.

A last boat was tethered to the slither of remaining platform. Someone Orin recognized from West Tip was loading the remaining people into a boat. Grey-cloaked engineers mixed with brown-cloaked West Tippers and people from every part of the island. Everybody was working together. There was no hierarchy when everyone was having to deal with peril. *That was some good to come of all this, at least,* Orin thought ruefully. Orin was sure he even recognized Thetus Black and Denira Goldsmith there, although they'd removed their Core Engineer cloaks and were wearing civilian clothes.

When the last person was in the boat and it pushed off safely to sea, Orin, Ferelith and Cody turned to look back at Ironhold. The land had clearly sunk lower, and only a small walkway remained leading back to the Engineerium sector. The only towers left were now those in the centre.

Cody clung tightly to Orin's neck, her body badly battered. He had tried to make her go with the others on to a boat, but she wouldn't leave him.

"I hope you have a plan!" said Ferelith as they ran along the thin strip of remaining land, picking their way between the fallen buildings and cracks.

"I think we can still save it," Orin puffed. He wasn't sure how; he just knew he couldn't leave without trying.

Rocks fell away beneath their feet as they leapt forward, crashing into the hungry waves and sending up plumes of water that drenched them. Stumbling and falling, dragging each other upright again, they continued, while metal splintered and groaned, and glass shattered around them. Panting as they ran, they realized the Engineerium tower had finally fallen.

Orin's knees nearly gave way. The ground crumbled away in front of them.

"Jump!" they yelled together, as they leapt to the craggy patch where the Engineerium had once stood, heaving air into their lungs.

"We're all right," said Ferelith.

Orin looked up to see blood dripping down her

cheek. Ferelith's clothes were ripped, her arms scraped, hair plastered to her head, her clothes drenched and every part of her shivering.

He knew he must be in the same state, and he laughed in relief and disbelief. Gently, he prised Cody's small metal hands from around his neck and held her. Her eyes flashed intermittently; there were multiple errors. Something heavy settled in his stomach. He'd never seen her so weak.

The storm shifted and the cloud pressed down, becoming a misty howl circling them. A blackened and twisted nest of roots remained, and in the middle of it stood Commander Forge, her white cloak now torn and filthy, the spliced V symbol of Ironhold pinning it hanging by a thread, her hair dull and bedraggled.

"Orin Crowfall. You certainly have a knack for staying alive, don't you? Like Eros did, dear fellow." She tilted her head and smiled. "You know, that's something we have in common, too."

"We have *nothing* in common!" He lunged for her, but Ferelith pulled him back.

"What good will that do?" Ferelith hissed. "She's nothing now. Even her own Core has abandoned her."

"The Sentinel is on its way here, to me. Perhaps I should thank you, for getting rid of the rest of the Core. Now all the remaining life-light will be mine, and there will be enough to protect me, well, for *ages*. I will use the monster's seed to plant a new Eard! Yes, it will take time to gather more life-light, but I will manage it. And you? Well, when all of you will have turned to dust, I will endure, endless as time."

Unable to contain his rage, Orin shouted, "Did you ever stop to think it's not *how long* you live, but *how* that matters?"

Ferelith gave a satisfied nod of agreement.

But Forge's eyes were vacant steel. She wasn't even listening.

Orin searched the blackened roots for any sign of life. Then he saw a small patch of brown beneath. "Look! Maybe we can still help it."

"But how?" Ferelith asked.

"Remember how the Eard of Natura took life-light from Blaine and Attica? What if I can give it some of mine?"

"Orin, no!"

But he already had his hands on the last living

290

part of the Eard. "Take some of my life-light!" he willed. "Please!"

Cody put a hand to his arm. "It's too late," she said weakly. "I can feel it." She tapped her chest.

"How?"

"My seed."

Orin tried to swallow, but his throat felt as though hands grasped it. A terrible feeling had taken hold.

Cody nodded. "It's too late for Ironhold, but . . . there is a way. Take my seed, go to . . . another island and plant it. Grow a new Eard, a child of Ironhold. If you don't do it, who will?"

"But then you wouldn't be. . ." He stopped himself. It was too painful to think of losing his friend.

"Look at me. I'm not some sapling clinging to a rock. Even you can't fix this."

He shook his head emphatically. "Cody, that's a hard human *negative* to your idea. I *will* fix you, I promise." Then he noticed Ferelith staring agape at the encroaching water.

Like death in a storm, the light of the mechanical sea monster shone through the waves.

Commander Forge raised her arms in triumph. "It has come back!"

The mechanical sea monster punched through the waves, heading straight for Orin, Ferelith and Cody. Its razor-sharp fury focused on them.

All Orin could do was clasp Ferelith in terror with one hand and pull Cody tightly to his chest. As though coming from a distant place, he heard Forge's maniacal laugh.

Cody's eyes locked with Orin's. She opened her mouth and spoke five words, so quietly he barely heard them. "Everything will be all right."

Time slowed, stretching like infinite space before them as the sea monster reared. Water sprayed them with its prescient icy sting.

Orin looked up as its great mechanical jaw opened. Every muscle became lead as he braced.

But at the final moment, its gaze shifted. The mechanical sea monster lurched its body sideways.

It had changed direction.

Disbelief, then unbridled horror, distorted Forge's face. It was heading for *her*. Iron teeth, sharp as swords, glinted, and Forge's mouth dropped open to let out a scream that never came.

The sea monster engulfed Ironhold's leader into its mouth, then continued its arc back through the exploding spray of the waves. It split the surface and plunged down towards the depths of the sea.

Orin stared after it in shock, watching it disappear far below, and then, there was a flash of light, some sort of explosion in the deep, and he knew that the sea monster had self-destructed.

The storm abated as suddenly as a flame snuffed from a candle. In its place, sea fog hung, waiting.

Ferelith scrambled to her feet and scanned the sea all around. "Where's it gone?"

With a bolt to his chest, Orin realized that Cody wasn't moving.

"Cody?"

Her body was limp. Her chest cavity was open, and in her hand, pulled from within, was the seed. It fell to the floor.

No! This couldn't be happening. Orin had spent every day of the last three years with Cody as his best friend – how could she just be gone? "I need tools, we can reconnect it—"

Ferelith bent down to pick up the seed and shook

her head. "Her body is in no state, and we have no tools. Perhaps ... perhaps she was right. We take the seed, the last of the Eard of Ironhold, and start again."

Tears pooled in Orin's eyes. "Cody's gone, Ferelith! What was it all for, if I couldn't even save my best friend? After everything we went through, we failed!" The reality of Cody being gone wouldn't register. If only he could turn back time and do things differently; perhaps there had been some way to fix things that he'd missed. Clutching her body, he half expected her to open her eyes and give him a sarcastic comment about humans being so easy to fool. But she was cold and utterly still. "I failed," he said weakly. Losing his best friend felt like losing a part of his own soul.

"No, Orin! There was nothing more we could have done." Warily, Ferelith glanced at the mist, and the crashing waves coming ever closer as the land sank.

The small piece of earth left began vibrating. Ferelith grasped the glowing seed.

The ground rumbled again. The last part of Ironhold was about to collapse, and there weren't any boats in sight.

Ferelith took Orin's hand. He squeezed it gratefully. "I think it's your turn for a plan."

"Technically, you're still captain of this adventure." Her voice wobbled.

All that remained of the great island of Ironhold was a tiny, craggy rock, which was about to sink into the sea, and two children sitting atop, trembling with the weight of the fear they had felt.

"Was this ocean adventure everything you hoped for?" Orin smiled nervously.

"It's certainly not been boring."

"We'll have to swim for it."

"Again? When I'm captain, which is in a few moments' time, then we're going to do things differently."

"The boats won't be far," Orin said. But inside he was exhausted, and he wasn't sure either of them would have the strength to make it. If Cody was here, she would be telling him he could do it, but who was going to have faith in him now?

He called out to the mist. "Help! Is there anyone out there?"

No one replied.

CHAPTER 25

Orin and Ferelith were up to their knees in rising water, about to take the plunge and swim as far as their strength allowed, when a large shape loomed out of the mist.

"That's not a boat," Orin breathed. Slowly it became clearer. It was an enormous head, and behind it, a large dome of moss and trees. It seemed to be smiling sympathetically at them. It blinked.

"It's the turtle island!" called Ferelith. They both squealed in delight.

The turtle submerged its head a little, allowing them to step on and climb on to its back. Ferelith went first, clutching Cody's seed close to her chest, and Orin then passed her Cody's body. He could hardly look at Cody. It was all so painful. Ferelith placed the fixie gently in the foliage, then pulled Orin up too.

They watched as the last of Ironhold crumbled beneath the waves for ever. Orin felt numb. It was the end of a chapter in his life, and he knew the only way forward was to move on. Then the turtle turned towards south and started to paddle.

The pair sank on to the mossy shell-ground at their feet. It was warm, and for the first time in weeks, Orin felt safe, despite the aching loss of Cody. They lay in silence for a while, both trying to take in the enormity of the past week or so.

"Orin! Ferelith!" someone called out of the mist.

Orin recognized the voice. "Grandpa?" he called. They both sat up as a boat came into sight.

Grandpa's beaming face looked up at them. "Well, I never!" He clutched the juniper sapling in one arm.

"I'm so glad you're all right! Are there many other boats out there? Are Mum and Dad safe?" Orin asked, his stomach squeezing with hope.

Grandpa nodded. "They're fine, and there are hundreds of boats. They're gathering in a chain.

But we don't know where to go. Perhaps your turtle island knows?"

Ferelith jumped up. "Orin, I do believe *I'm* captain now. We head south for Natura!" she called. She picked up the seed from the ground, shimmering like a precious jewel, and squeezed Orin's arm. "All is not lost."

Despite the ache in Orin's heart for Cody, his family was all right, and they had the seed. He knew now that no matter how bad things got, there was always light to be found in the darkness. He smiled sadly as he remembered Cody's last words to him and said, "Everything will be all right."

After they bid thanks and farewell to the giant turtle, it took a day and a night to sail to Natura. After the mechanical sea monster had taken Commander Forge, and the Eard of Ironhold was no longer in pain, the storms calmed. Orin knew that slowly, nature would begin to heal. And maybe his heart would heal, too.

Nara, Thao and some others from the island awaited them on the north beach, having spotted them on the horizon.

Nara hurried into the waves to greet them, a rare smile illuminating her face. "You're back! And you've brought quite a few people with you." Ferelith and Nara hugged each other tightly, and Thao joined them.

Ferelith turned to her uncle. "I'm sorry, I know you don't like outsiders, but these people have nowhere else to go," she said, her voice commanding, as though anticipating resistance.

Thao held her shoulders. "The Eard has been like a different island since you left. Come. You are all welcome."

Orin and his family stayed with Thao and Ferelith in Heart Tree. It was strange for Orin to see his family experiencing the Eard of Natura for the first time, and Grandpa asked question after question of Thao, who seemed to take a particular liking to him and showed him around the village. Saviri, although wary at first, was curious to learn about how things had been on Ironhold, and was soon outraged at how West Tippers had been treated and insisted on filling Orin's parents with all the good food she could find. Nara told Orin and Ferelith about all the work she'd led, including setting up some growing spaces to nurture independent seeds and plants, and plans for making mechanical fruit pickers for their home trees. Thao had decided that the rituals would be less frequent and optional, and that punishments would be assigned and executed by humans only. Apparently this announcement had also triggered a wave of sweet-scented blossoms from the Eard all over the island.

Later, Orin, Ferelith, Nara and Thao sat on the outside roots of Heart Tree in the evening sun.

"Since you and Orin left, we worked through the changes here to take pressure off the Eard, and to show it that it doesn't have to control us in order to protect itself," said Nara. "We're learning to look after ourselves a bit more. Even my mother has decided to start growing her own vegetables on the south side of the island! We're getting used to some new tools, but it's all running much more . . . harmoniously."

Orin was glad that things were working out on Natura, but his heart ached seeing how things could have been on Ironhold, and that Cody wasn't here to see it all. Sometimes he found himself looking down at his side, expecting her to still be there.

Thao stroked his thick brown beard. "So, what's next? You are all welcome to stay. There is plenty for all."

Orin looked at the seed in his hand. "We're going to plant this. I was thinking of the island we stopped at on the way back to Ironhold. It was uninhabited and had some good natural resources. Except..."

"Except?" frowned Ferelith.

"Well, how do we decide on a leader? Not like before, of course; someone fair and balanced. Someone to bring everyone together – like you, Thao."

"Why not *you*?" asked Ferelith, grinning.

"Oh, no, it could never be me! I'm just a kid, I'm not even an engineer..."

Ferelith tutted. "Stop thinking about who you *think* you are. Be the person I've always seen. The person Cody knew you were. The boy who washed up on the beach and survived. The boy who stood up to the Eard of Natura, who crossed oceans to save his people. Who stood up to Commander Forge."

"You'll make a fine leader, Orin Crowfall." Thao smiled. "Go to that island. Plant that seed, before I cast you into the sea myself."

In his heart, Orin knew Ferelith was right. Commander Forge made the wrong choices, but it didn't mean that he would. Wasn't it time to just be who he was inside? The person who loved growing, nurturing and protecting.

"What about you?"

Ferelith smiled. "I'm free to do the thing I've always longed for; to find adventure."

"As long as you come back to visit," said Thao. "We welcome outsiders now. Island communities are better working together than surviving on their own."

Orin's heart sank at the thought of Ferelith leaving. He had hoped she might want to come with him to the new island.

Her green eyes burned brightly as she nudged him. "You realize that by new shores I mean I'm tagging along with you." She paused. "Unless you don't want me to."

"How else am I going to keep myself in – I mean, *out* – of trouble?" He beamed.

While most of the Ironholders preferred to stay at Natura, exploring and enjoying its eye-popping bounty, some of the people from Ironhold decided to sail with Orin and Ferelith to the new island. Many of his parents' West Tip friends and some of the cultivators were eager to help grow crops and establish a brand-new home. The disgraced engineers of the Core who had survived were to stay on Natura under the supervision of Thao.

Orin's parents and Grandpa sailed in one of the larger boats, while Orin and Ferelith sailed together. For a long while, there was a comfortable silence as the pair navigated the waters, safe in the knowledge that as companions, they shared the wounds of what had happened and the excitement of what might lie ahead.

Eventually their destination came into view.

The island was storm-worn on the northern coast, ravaged by the Ironhold-induced gales. But a freshwater stream ran down in rivulets on to the rocky beach, so there would be sufficient freshwater, and Orin was delighted that the black soil he found further inland crumbled easily between his fingers, ideal for planting. Orin and Ferelith hiked to where they judged the very centre of the island to be and dug a hole, then gently planted the seed of the Eard.

They both stood back.

"Now what?" asked Orin.

"We nurture it, that's what." Ferelith pulled out her notebook and showed him what she'd been working on. "Look – I've sketched some structures we could build, so we don't have to rely too much on the Eard, but we can protect it and give it space to flourish. And in the meantime, we have the seeds and cuttings the Ironholders thought to save, to begin our own first crops."

"These drawings are really good."

"Thanks. Also, we should think of a name for the island."

"I think I know what it should be," Orin said thoughtfully. He'd been pondering it on the journey over. "I want it to stand for something, to represent finding a new way to live. This island is about being who you want to be, choosing your own dreams and hopes in a fresh start. That's what's brought me here, and that's the sort of place I want to create. So how about the island of Genesis?"

Ferelith smiled. "It's perfect."

They headed back to the beach area, where everyone else was setting up shelters. Orin found that he was starting to think differently, that he wasn't seeing them as engineers, or cultivators, or West Tippers. Now they were all pioneers, together.

Grandpa patted Orin on the back. He handed Orin a parcel wrapped with a large leaf and tied with vine. "An early birthday present. Excuse the wrapping."

Orin unwrapped it. "Grandma's book! You saved it."

"I couldn't leave Ironhold without it. Mind, there's a new tale to add to the pages now, though. And surely more to come."

"Thanks, Grandpa."

"You're welcome, my boy. Grandma would've been so proud of you." He ruffled Orin's hair, then stretched back in the sunshine. "I reckon I'm going to enjoy my days here."

A dark patch in the sky caught Orin's eye. Not another storm, surely?

Or could it be. . .

Heart leaping, Orin ran to a nearby tree and clambered to the top. He drew a lungful of salty breeze, spread his arms wide to feel it on his fingertips, and took in the wonder before his eyes.

It wasn't a cloud – not the usual kind, anyway. It was a cloud of birds. Crows! A whole flock of them. They circled the island, then landed in the trees around him, their joyful *carks* echoing through the air. One landed close to Orin, and his heart nearly stopped. There was something so wise and knowing about the bird's expression, and in its eyes Orin thought he could actually see adventure, far-off lands, and – could it be – forgiveness?

Perhaps it was a trick of the light. Or perhaps the bird's eyes merely reflected Orin's own expression.

Ferelith called up to him, "Hey, Orin Crowfall. I think that's what you call destiny!"

He smiled.

The tale of Orin Crowfall could be anything he wanted it to be.

EPILOGUE

ONE YEAR LATER

Ferelith was fishing with Orin's mum. The young girl had quickly become the best sailor on the island; she repeatedly beat Orin in races and went off for the odd week or two to explore the sea, find new islands and chart the ocean.

Orin didn't mind, though. He was busy nurturing the fields, orchards, the juniper and the Eard of Genesis, which was thriving with a Heart Tree now twice as tall as Orin. The roots had taken hold well, and all manner of creatures had come to live on the island since they'd planted it, including some relflings who flew in on the breeze, some honeybees who were happily making a hive on the north of Genesis, and some long-eared, fluffy creatures with leaf-like wings, who seemed to pair with individual humans and enjoy nestling on their feet to keep warm in the evenings. The waels were regular visitors to the shores, and the turtle island would pop by to give the occasional ride to islanders. The crow colony was thriving too and lived in harmony with the people. As Orin got to know them, they had become like friends, and he'd realized how intelligent they were. He observed them making tools by fashioning twigs into spears and hooks, then using them to eat grubs. They were also excellent at keeping rodents in check and stopping them from taking too many grains.

Every week, Grandpa gathered all the children of the island to visit the Eard. It had become known as "Story Time with the Eard". Ferelith would tell stories of the new places she had discovered at sea, and Grandpa and Orin would tell Tales of Beyond, which included stories of other islands and the oceans, what had come before, and what had happened to Ironhold. Grandpa said it would help the children grow up to understand the world with all its joys and its perils. Orin would let them put their hands to the Eard so that they would grow to understand its feelings, as it would theirs. It was one of his favourite parts of the week. When their tiny hands made contact with the ever-growing Heart Tree, beautiful blossoms of white grew around their fingers.

Orin was about to head off to check on the evening meal when something caught his eye in the small Heart Tree of the Eard. Something round and glowing that fizzled with light. He stared in wonder, his heart beating fast. Could it be?

Ferelith charged through the trees. "You missed a treat today! A pod of dolphins sailed beside us, and..." She stopped beside him and looked up.

He grabbed her hand and squeezed. "Look, Ferelith! I'm not seeing things, am I?" He'd been waiting and hoping for this moment since they'd arrived.

The branch growing the seed extended towards him.

Ferelith nudged him. "It's offering it to you!"

Slowly, Orin reached out his hand and took the seed, then he bowed respectfully to the Eard in thanks. He and Ferelith looked at each other, smiled, then whooped for joy because they knew what this meant.

They ran back to Orin's shelter.

The metallic body of a fixie lay on a table. Orin had repaired Cody's body and antennae as best he could, using the tools they had. He'd even made some new wings. Carefully, he opened the chest panel and set about attaching the wires. His hands shook. He paused.

"What if it doesn't work? What if she's not who she was any more? What if—" He'd hoped for so long, he didn't think he could bear it if Cody came back as anything other than herself.

Ferelith rolled her eyes. "Just do it."

He attached the last wire and carefully closed her chest panel.

Nothing happened.

"Maybe I did it wrong." Orin's heart was thumping wildly. Why wasn't it working?

"Believe," said Ferelith.

Slowly, the fixie's lips parted. Her eyes flashed to life.

They peered at her.

"Can you hear us?" asked Orin.

"Affirmative," she said robotically.

His heart sank. It was standard fixie language.

"Affirmative that you still need lessons in believing in yourself, Orin Crowfall." Cody winked.

Ferelith laughed and Orin wiped a tear from his eye. He felt like he might burst with happiness. "It's really you!" Orin spread his hands out to the woven shelter. "It's not much, but—"

"—it's home," Cody finished. She pushed herself up on her elbows. Her wings fluttered behind her. "Well, that's a welcome improvement!" She looked between them. "I'm me, but are you really *you*? You're both somewhat stretched since last time . . . and do you both have . . . suntans?"

"Yes, Cody, the answer to that is. . ."

And then they all said, "Affirmative!"

ACKNOWLEDGEMENTS

I would like to thank various kind and talented people for their help in the journey of this story. Firstly, and pivotally, Imogen Cooper for believing in me and the concept some years back, even though I hadn't found the right way to tell the story yet. Also, Kate Shaw, Linas Alsenas, Jenny Glencross, Jamie Gregory, George Ermos, and Pete Matthews for working their usual outstanding magic.

This is my fifth novel from Scholastic UK, and an opportune moment to express my thanks to the entire Scholastic UK children's books team in all the departments, whom do such a wonderful job with my books. Thank you for all your support.

Vashti Hardy is the author of *Brightstorm* and its sequel, *Darkwhispers*, as well as *Wildspark*, winner of the Blue Peter Book Awards Best Story 2020. *Brightstorm* has been translated into several languages, was selected for Independent Booksellers Book of the Season and Primary School Book Club Reads, won the West Sussex Children's Story Book Award and was shortlisted for the Waterstones Children's Book Prize, Books are My Bag Awards and Leeds Book Award. She is also the author of *Harley Hitch and the Iron Forest*, for younger readers.

Twitter @vashti_hardy
Instagram vashtihardyauthor